A Second Love

A Love Lost A Love Found

Sharon Allen

A Second Love

A Love Lost A Love Found

Published by Adriel Publishing

FIRST EDITION

Printed in the U.S.A.

Cover design by Sharon Allen

ISBN: 978-1-892324-54-2

Acknowledgment

To John Phillips, who served his country as a Marine. Thank you for helping me with my Marine, Jimmy.

Dedication

For my brother Mike. You have always been there for me.

I love you

Sis

Chapter 1

Sitting in the back seat of Jimmy's old Ford, Sandy and Jimmy are parked at their favorite spot at the lake. The lake is alive with night sounds, and the moon is reflecting a beautiful hue through the moving waves from the wind.

They lovingly reminisce about their days in school together and all the fun they have had over the years.

"Are you sure you want to marry me? Even though I have a good job, I don't have much money. It's going to be hard to make it for a while," said Jimmy.

"Oh, honey, listen. I told you money doesn't matter. I love you," Sandy replied. "We can make it because we love each other. Besides, I have my job at the drug store. It will be enough."

Jimmy looked down at his watch. "Oh gosh, Sandy, I didn't realize it was so late. Your parents are going to kill me. I better get you home." He takes her in his arms and romantically kisses her. – a long kiss. They begrudgingly climb over the seat and give each other one more hug. Jimmy slowly takes out his keys and starts the engine. He grabs for her hand as they make the slow drive back to Sandy's home.

Chapter 2

A month after graduation, Sandra's mother is getting the invitations ready to send out. "Sandra, you need to look at this list and make sure you haven't left anyone out. The wedding is in two weeks, so I need to get them mailed."

"Okay, Mom. I'll be right down," Sandra calls to her mother. "Jimmy, I've got to go. Mom is waiting for me to check the list for the wedding. I'm so excited. I'm going to be your wife in just two weeks. I can't wait. I love you. I'll call you later."

Sandy glided down the steps to the living room where her mother was holding up an invitation.

"Sandy, you know your father is not ready to let go of his little girl. We both wish you would wait. You're both so young. But I don't want you to run off and elope. I'd rather you get married here with your family."

"I know, Mom, but we love each other. Jimmy has a steady job at the garage, and I'm going to work at the drug store while I go to night school to work on my college degree. We have thought it all out."

"Mom, please don't worry. We'll still be close. Our apartment is just a couple of blocks away. Jimmy's parents have said they are going to give us some furniture, and the apartment already has a fridge and a stove. We won't have to put out any extra money for appliances."

Sandy sifted through all of the paperwork on the dining room table. "Now, where is the list?" She carefully looks through all of the names on the invitation list.

It looks okay. Jimmy said his aunt and uncle are going to come to town for the wedding. I can't think of anything else. The dress you and dad bought for me is so pretty. I can't wait for Jimmy to see me in it. Do you think Aunt Mary and Uncle John will be able to come? I know she hasn't been feeling well," Sandra rambled on.

"I talked to her yesterday, and she said they are coming. You know she's the reason you're so spoiled. Since they never had any kids, she treated you like you were hers."

Sandy lovingly looked at her mom "I know, but you're my favorite mother."

Her mother laughed. "I'm your *only* mother."

"That's why you're my favorite." Sandy kisses her mother on the cheek. "I've got to go. Sally wants to show me her maid of honor dress. I'll be back in time to help with dinner."

Chapter 3

"Hey, Sandy, come on in. I want to try my dress on for you. Mom helped me pick it out. It's upstairs." Sally turns and runs up the stairs with Sandy following.

Sally leaves Sandy sitting on the bed and goes into the bathroom to put on the dress. "What do you think?" Sally asks as she steps out. "Isn't it gorgeous?"

"I love it. That color blue is perfect. It looks great on you. Wait until Max sees you in it. He'll go crazy. When are you two going to get married?"

"I promised my mom and dad that I would at least go to college for one year before we do. They think if I get away from Max, I'll be so busy I'll forget about him and especially about getting married. They like Max. They just don't want me getting married so young."

Sandy nodded. "My parents aren't thrilled about us getting married either. They don't want us to elope. So they decided to give in. I'm so excited. I can't wait to be Mrs. Jimmy Thompson. It's just two weeks away!"

Sally jealously looked over at Sandy. "No, Max is relentless; he wants to elope and he keeps trying to talk me into it, but I'm afraid. If my mom and dad found out, I don't know what they would do. I do love him."

Sally changed the subject. "Did you get that apartment you wanted?"

"Yes, Jimmy put the deposit down yesterday. You and Max will have to come over when we get moved in."

Sally goes over to her dresser and gets a little box. "I got you something for your something new. It's not much, but I think you'll like it."

Sandy opens the little box and finds a bracelet with two hearts on it.

"Oh Sally, this is beautiful. You are my best friend ever, but you shouldn't have spent so much money." She hugs Sally. "I will wear it forever. I remember when we met at the bus stop. That was the first day of Junior high school. We had just moved here, and I didn't know anyone. You asked me to sit down with you on the bus. We have been friends ever since."

"Yeah, you looked so lost. I'm glad I asked you to sit down. It's hard to move to another place and not know anyone. I guess I better take this dress off before I mess it up. Are you going to stay for dinner?"

"No, I promised Mom I would be home in time for dinner, so I guess I better go. Are you and Max going to the movies with us this Saturday?"

"If he doesn't have to work. I hope so."

"Okay, see you later. Call me and let me know if you all are going to be able to join us Saturday."

Chapter 4

"Mom, Jimmy is coming over, and we're going to the movies with Sally and Max. I finished with the dishes. Is there anything else you want me to do before I leave?"

"No, sweetie. Oh, your dad wanted to talk to you before Jimmy gets here."

"Dad?"

"I'm in the den, Sandy. I heard you say you're going to the movies with Jimmy. I need to ask you something. I know you're about to get married, but I hope if you and Jimmy are, ah, getting intimate, you're careful. You don't want to start a family this early. I wish you would wait and think about finishing college, but I guess you're old enough to make up your own mind." He looks down at the newspaper in his lap. "You're my little girl, and you will always be my little girl."

Sandy goes over and sits in his lap. "I know Daddy, I love you. You'll always be my favorite man. Jimmy will have to settle for being my second favorite." She hugs him, then kisses him on the cheek. "Got to go now. I need to change before he gets here."

Later, after picking up Sally and Max, they head to the movie. "Let's go to the drive-in. That new monster movie is showing. It's supposed to be scary." Max leans over the seat.

"What do you think?"

"Sounds good," Jimmy replies.

Half way through the movie, Max has his arm around Sally. "I sure would like to be with you. "He whispers in her ear. "You know I love you. If your mother and daddy would let us, we could get married like Jimmy and Sandy."

"I love you too, Max, and I want to, but I'm afraid. I think we better wait until I come back from my first year at college. You *are* going to wait for me, aren't you?"

"Yes, I'll wait for you. I don't want anyone else. It's okay. I just want you awfully bad. You're the only girl for me."

After the movie, they take the girls home then as Max is getting out of the car, he turns and asks Jimmy, "Have you and Sandy, you know, been together yet? I know you're getting married, and all. I want Sally, but she is scared and wants to wait until she gets back from her first year at college."

"If Sally isn't ready, you should wait like she wants you to."

"Yeah, you're right. Okay, see you."

Chapter 5

The two weeks fly by and the day of the wedding is here. Sally is upstairs, getting ready with Sandy.

"I can't believe you're getting married. You're so lucky. I wish it was me and Max."

"You'll only have to wait a year like you promised your mother and dad. The time will speed by. You can still see Max when you come home on break."

"I know, I'm just jealous. Are you ready to put on your wedding dress? I'll brush your hair for you when you get it on. That way, your hair won't get messed up. Then we can put on your veil."

"Mom is going to come up and help us finish. She is not sure if she is sad or happy. She gave me a handkerchief that daddy gave to her a long time ago. I have your bracelet for something new. Aunt Mary gave me a blue garter, and you loaned me your favorite earrings for something borrowed." Sandy pulls her wedding dress from its cover and slips it on. She turns to look in the mirror.

"Sandy, you look simply beautiful. Jimmy is going to flip out. You're going to be so happy." Sally wipes some tears from her eyes.

"Don't start that, or I'll cry and mess up my makeup."

Sandy's mother opens the door and stops. "You look like a model out of a magazine, but prettier. Is there anything I can do to help?"

"You can do this top button for me. I can't reach it. I think as soon as I put on the veil, we'll both be ready. Is Dad ready?"

"Yes, and he looks so good in his new suit. He is waiting at the top of the stairs for you. Everyone is here. Jimmy looks nice in his suit, and so does his best man, Max. Sally, you look beautiful; that blue is perfect for you."

"Thank you, Mrs. Taylor, you look great too."

"Well, I'll get your dad, and I'll be downstairs. I love you, little girl. I know you and Jimmy will be happy. Just remember if you ever need us, we'll be here. No matter what." She kisses Sandy on the cheek and then hugs Sally.

Chapter 6

There is a knock on the door, and her dad opens it. He looks at Sandy and gets tears in his eyes. "Jimmy is getting the most beautiful girl in the world. I hope he knows how lucky he is. Are you ready?" He hugs her, then puts his arm out for her to take. Sally leads the way down the stairs as the music begins to play the wedding march.

Sally enters the living room and starts toward the front where the preacher and Jimmy are waiting. Max is at his side. As Sandy and her dad enter, everyone stands. They get to the front, and her dad gives her hand to Jimmy. "Take care of my baby," her dad tells him.

Jimmy takes her hand and says, "Yes, sir, for the rest of my life."

"Jimmy and Sandy have written their vows to each other. Sandy, would you please say your vows to Jimmy?" the preacher asks.

"Jimmy, I know we're both young to be married, but you are all I have ever wanted. I will be a good wife to you, faithful and honest. I will put you first in everything I do. My love will never waver; it will be strong and will last until the day I die."

The preacher looks over at Jimmy. "Jimmy, will you please say your vows to Sandy?"

"Sandy, I have loved you ever since that first time I saw you in the hall in fifth grade. I decided I would marry you that day. You have made me the happiest man in the world by becoming my wife. I will love and cherish you and be faithful to you until the day I die."

After they are pronounced husband and wife, he kisses her, and everyone applauds. The reception is small, with just a cake and some punch. Her mom cries as they get ready to leave. Her dad gets Jimmy aside and gives him a hundred dollars. "This is a wedding gift from her mom and me. Welcome to the family, Jimmy. Just take care of our Sandy."

Jimmy's parents had given them two nights at the Center Hotel, the best hotel in town. They say their goodbyes and leave in his old Ford with *JUST MARRIED* painted on the back window and tin cans streaming from the bumper.

Chapter 7

"This room is so nice. I've never stayed in a hotel before. Your mom said this was the honeymoon suite. Look at all the flowers."

"I'm too busy looking at my beautiful wife." He pulls her close and kisses her. "I can't believe we're married. I love you so much." He picks her up and takes her to the bedroom. He puts her down and takes off his coat.

"I need to freshen up first. Will you get my little suitcase and put it in the bathroom for me?" Sandra asks.

"Don't be too long," he says with a smile.

"You'll just have to wait." She closes the door and opens her suitcase. Looking in the mirror, she puts on the long white nightgown Sally had given her. All of a sudden, Sandra gets butterflies in her stomach.

She takes a deep breath and opens the door. He has turned out the lights. She feels relieved. She steps out and stands there.

"Wow! You look beautiful, Sandy." He pulls her into his arms and kisses her. Then he picks her up and gently lays her on the bed.

"We are free to make love without worry or feeling guilty for loving each other."

Later that night, they order room service. They spend the next day in and out of bed, learning about each other. They talk of going out to a movie but decide to curl up in the bed and watch TV. They can't seem to get enough of each other.

"I've never been so happy, Jimmy. We're married, we have our little apartment, and a whole life together" She leans over and puts her head on his shoulder.

"I know we're young, and your parents didn't want us to get married so soon. But we will prove everyone wrong. I will make you a good husband. I will work hard, and you will go to night school. Nothing will keep us from having a great life.

On the morning of the third day, they are getting ready to leave the suite. He walks into the bathroom, and she is just getting out of the shower. He wraps her towel around her and carries her to the bed. "I just want to show you one more time how much I love you before we go."

She laughs and kisses him as he lays her down on the bed.

Chapter 8

A few weeks go by. They are settling into their apartment. She enrolls in night school, and he is working hard at the garage. They are each learning to share their space with the other. The tiny bathroom is not big enough for two, but they seem to enjoy trying to squeeze by each other, and brushing their teeth at the same time is a challenge. Sandy gets up and fixes breakfast for Jimmy, and while he eats, she packs his lunch.

Their apartment is decorated with things people have given them and some things she has found at garage sales. They have their own little world, and each day is a new time together. Max and Sally come over often. Their friendship grows stronger each day. They depend on each other for advice. Mainly they just have fun together.

"Hello, Sandy, I need to talk to you. Can I come over."

"Of course, Sally, What's wrong? You sound like you've been crying. Jimmy isn't due home from work for a couple of hours. Come on over."

Sally knocks on the door. When Sandy opens it, she sees tears in Sally's eyes. Sally wraps her arms around her and cries. "Tell me what's wrong," Sandra demands. "You're scaring me."

"It's Max. He wants to make love to me before I go off to college. He says he is afraid I'll find someone else. He just wants to know I love him, but I don't know what to do. I love him. I'm just not ready to go that far. What should I do?'

"Sit down and let me get you some tea, then we can talk." Sandra brings two glasses of tea and sits down on the couch with Sally. "I can't tell you what to do. You have to decide for yourself. I know you and Max love each other, but if you aren't ready, don't let him push you into it. Whether you make love or not, is not going to keep you from meeting someone else at college. If Max loves you like he says he does, he will wait. You need to do what do you feel in your heart is right for you?"

"I don't know. I don't want to lose him. I'm just not ready to go that far

"Then that's your answer. Do what you feel is right for you."

"I guess I just had to hear myself say it out loud. Thanks, Sandy. You're my best friend. I couldn't talk to anyone else about this."

Chapter 9

Jimmy comes in the door with a dozen roses. “Hello, Beautiful,” he says and hands them to Sandy. “You didn’t think I would forget our three months anniversary, did you?”

“I didn’t know we would celebrate until it had been six months. But I’m not complaining. These are beautiful; let me get a vase for them.” She comes back with them in a glass vase. “ I did get you a card, though, and a new shirt.” She reaches behind the couch and pulls up a box with a card stuck in the ribbon.

“You’re sneaky. I didn’t think you would think about it.” He opens up the box and finds a blue striped shirt and then reads the card.

To the most wonderful husband in the world, you will be my love forever. I love you. Sandy

“This is the best present I’ve ever gotten. No, You’re the best present I’ve ever gotten. I hope you haven’t started anything for dinner. I want to take you to that new Mexican restaurant in town.”

“That sounds like fun. I’ve heard their food is great. Give me a few minutes to change.” She kisses him and starts toward the bedroom.

He comes up behind her and picks her up and tosses her on the bed. “They are open late tonight since it’s Friday.” He laughs and leaps on the bed next to her.

She looks up at him and says, “I’m not hungry right now, but I will be later.”

A couple of hours later, they make it to the restaurant and are waiting for a table. She feels someone tap her on the shoulder. She looks around and sees her mother and daddy standing in line behind them. “Hey, you two. Are you meeting anyone for dinner?”

“No, we’re not. Why don’t you sit with us? You know this is our three-month anniversary. So we decided to celebrate.”

“Congratulations, but we don’t want to intrude.”

“Please join us,” Jimmy says. “You can help us celebrate.”

“If you’re sure, we would love to.”

Dinner is great. There is a lot of laughter. Sandy’s mom and dad tell some embarrassing stories about Sandy when she was young, but she is a good sport about it. After dinner, Jimmy asks the waiter for the check, but her dad has already taken care of it. They kiss goodbye and head for home.

Chapter 10

Sandy gets a call in the middle of the day from the garage where Jimmy works. "Sandy, this is Mel, Jimmy's boss. Jimmy has gotten hurt. "

"How? Is he okay? What happened?"

'The jack on one of the cars gave way, and the bumper came down on his leg. I'm on my way to the hospital with him. He wanted me to call you so you can meet us there."

"Tell him I'm on my way. Is it bad?"

"I don't think so. It might be broken, but I'm no doctor. We'll see you there."

Sandy gets there just as Mel pulls up with Jimmy. The emergency people come out with a gurney for Jimmy. She rushes up to him and takes his hand. "I'm here, Jimmy."

They take him in and ask her and Mel to sit in the waiting room while they do some x-rays to see the damage. Sandy paces the room, and Mel asks her if he can get her anything.

"No, thank you. I hope it's not too bad. Thank you for bringing him in and calling me."

She calls Jimmy's parents. "Mrs. Johnson, this is Sandy."

"Yes, ma'am, I'm okay. But Jimmy had an accident at work, and I'm at the hospital with him. A jack broke and I think his leg is broken."

"Yes ma'am. I'm in the waiting room, right when you come through the emergency door. I'll be waiting there."

She thinks maybe she should call her mom and dad. "Hello, Mom. Jimmy has been hurt. We're at the hospital. It may be a broken leg. I'm waiting for the doctor. I called his mom and dad and they are on their way. You don't have to come, but I would like it if you did. I'm really scared."

"Thanks mom. See you in a few minutes."

It seems like hours. Everyone is waiting for the doctor to come out and tell them what is happening.

Finally, the double doors open, and the doctor comes toward them. "Mrs. Johnson?"

Sandy and his mother both stand up. Sandy says, "I'm his wife. Is he okay?"

"His leg is not broken; it's just badly bruised. He's going to be okay. He will have to take it easy for a while. He needs to stay off it for at least a week. He will be able to go home in a few minutes. They are filling out his papers now."

Sandy hugs her mother. "He's going to be okay. I'll take good care of him."

"Don't worry about the bill. I've taken care of it." Mel, Jimmy's boss, hugs Sandy. "Just make sure Jimmy takes care of himself. He has a pretty nurse anyway. He'll get paid while he is off. That's why we have insurance." Mel says goodbye and leaves.

Chapter 11

In a few minutes, they bring Jimmy out in a wheelchair with his leg propped up . Sandy runs to him and kisses him. "I was so worried about you. I would die if something happened to you."

"I'm okay. It's just bruised. You're not going to get rid of me that easily."

"Don't joke. You could have been seriously hurt," Sandy scolds.

"Are you going to be able to get him home? We can go with you and help you get him settled. He will need some crutches. We can stop by the drug store and get him some."

"Thanks, Mr. Johnson, that would be great. Getting him in the house is going to be hard by myself."

Sandy's mother looks over at them, "Why don't you and Mrs. Johnson go-ahead to their house and help him get settled? We'll get the crutches for him and meet you there."

"That sounds like a good idea. Thanks. Please call us Stan and Nancy."

Sandy's mother replied, "Only if you call us Harry and Judy. It's a plan then. We'll see you all at the kids' house."

"Thanks, mom and dad. I don't know what I'd do without the four of you." She hugs everyone and turns to Jimmy. “You ready to go? I’ll go bring the car around. Mel got someone to come and get him so he could leave our car here.” She kissed him. “Don’t go anywhere. “

“HA! HA! You’re funny.” He laughed.

Chapter 12

When they got home, Jimmy's dad helped him into the house and onto the couch. He propped his leg up on a pillow. "Is that okay? Does it feel comfortable?"

"As much as it can be. It hurts some. They gave me a shot for pain, but it will take a while to help."

Sandy came in with a pitcher of tea and some glasses. "Thought we could all use something to drink."

"Thank you, Sandy. You have fixed up your apartment really nice. It's very homey."

"Thank you, Mrs. Johnson. The kitchen table and chairs you gave us are nice, and they go good with everything."

"Hello, can we come in? We got the crutches and also stopped by the drive in and got some burgers. It's lunch time, and none of us have eaten."

"That's great Dad. I'm starving. I made some tea, so we're all set."

Chapter 13

The next morning Jimmy sits with his leg propped up in his recliner. Sandy is busy in the kitchen when someone knocks on the door. Jimmy hobbles to answer it.

“Hey, what are you doing up? Aren’t you supposed to be taking it easy?

“Hey, Max. What’s going on? I haven’t seen you in a couple of weeks. Have you heard from Sally? I think she’s coming in next week.”

“Nah, I haven’t talked to her. I’ve been seeing someone else.”

“Are you serious? I thought you and Sally were going to get married after she finished a year of college. What happened?”

Sandy comes in and sees Max. “Hello, Max.” The words come out very cold.

“Hello, Sandy. How are you?”

“I’m fine. I’ve got some things to do in the kitchen.” She walks off.

“ I guess she has talked to Sally. It’s obvious she doesn’t want to talk to me.”

Jimmy looks concerned, “What happened between the two of you? You were so close.”

“After Sally left for college, I met this girl at a party. She’s hot! And she likes to party. Do you know what I mean? We hit it off, and I’ve been seeing her a lot. I guess it got back to Sally and she wrote me a letter and broke up with me. I guess she just wasn't the girl for me. She is kind of immature."

"I can't believe you. You said you loved her. I guess your version of love and mine are different. You're a creep, Max. Sally deserves better than you. I think you need to leave. I don't blame Sandy for not wanting to talk to you. I don't either."

"I thought you'd understand. You being a guy. Guess I was wrong. See you."

After he leaves, Sandy comes back in. "Did he tell you? Sally is lucky she didn't do what he wanted her to. He's a creep."

"That's what I told him. He won't be back. I don't want friends like that. I hope Sally knows she is welcome here."

"She does. I knew you would feel that way. You're a good man, and you know what's right and what's wrong. I guess Max doesn't. That's why I love you."

Chapter 14

A year passes, Jimmy is back at work Sandy is still going to night school, they are planning for Christmas. They have invited both of their parents for Christmas Dinner. They have decorated their tree, and apartment with all things Christmas. Sandy is cooking her first big dinner for their parents.

"Do you think there is going to be enough? I can get more if I need to."

"Sandy, you have enough for an army. It's going to be great. Mom is going to bring the pies, and your mom is bringing the turkey. All we have to do is furnish the rest. The table looks great, and you have the apartment all decorated. Don't be so nervous, it's just our parents."

"I know, I just want everything to go well. This is our first big family event. I want them to see how happy we are and how good we're doing. They know, sweetheart."

"That must be them. I'll get it. You look very pretty, too. I love you, Mrs. Johnson."

"I love you, too, Mr. Johnson. Okay, I'm ready."

"Sandy, you look so pretty. And your apartment looks so cheery with all the decorations. Where do you want me to put the pies?" Mrs. Johnson asks.

“Just put them in the kitchen on the counter. They sure look good.”

Sandy’s parents walk in. “Anybody home? Is this where the Christmas party is?”

Jimmy runs to the door. “Yes, it is. Come on in, Mr. and Mrs. Taylor. Wow! That’s a big turkey. Looks good. Just set it in the middle of the table. We have a few things to bring in from the kitchen. All of you have a seat while we finish setting the table.”

“Can we help?”

“No, we got it, thanks.”

After dinner with the dishes done, they sit in front of the tree and open presents. When they are all opened, Jimmy leaves the room and comes back in and hands Sandy a tiny velvet box. “ I didn’t have enough money to buy you an engagement ring when we got married, so I thought it was about time.”

“Oh, Jimmy, it’s beautiful.” She stands up and hugs him, then turns to show it to their parents. “I love it. The emerald is my favorite stone.

“I remembered how you told Sally once that the emerald was your favorite. That’s why I picked that one.”

Chapter 15

After Christmas, they settle back into their routine. Sandy is not far from getting her certificate from night school. Jimmy has gotten a raise and a promotion to head mechanic at the garage.

One evening Sandy gets a call from Sally, "Sandy, how is everything going? I didn't get to come home for Christmas. I had a really hard exam and had to study. I'm going to be there in a couple of weeks. I was wondering if I could come by and bring someone with me for you to meet? He's a really nice guy. I think I might be falling for him. I didn't know how you would feel about it since Max is a friend of Jimmy's."

"Not any longer. When he found out what Max did, he told him to leave. We both think he's a rat. We would love for you to bring your new guy to meet us. I'm glad you found someone who will treat you right. Just let us know when you will be in town. Can't wait to see you."

"Me too. Call you later."

Sandy excitedly yelled out to Jimmy. "Sally has a new guy. She wants to bring him by to meet us. I told her we would like to meet him. She was not sure because of Max being your friend. I told her he wasn't anymore; that you didn't like the way he treated Sally."

"I'm glad she got away from Max. Sally is a great girl and deserves to be treated right."

Chapter 16

Two weeks later Sally and Ronny come to visit. “Hey, Sally, glad you made it.”

“Sandy, this is Ronny. I met him in my English class.”

“Glad to meet you, Ronny. Jimmy will be home in a few minutes. Come on in and sit down. Is this your first year too.”

“No, this is my second. I’m after an associate degree in Finance. You have a great apartment. Sally has told me a lot about you and Jimmy. You two are best friends since grade school.”

“Yeah. She was my maid of honor when we got married. We were as close as sisters growing up. Where ever you would find one of us, the other was there too. So you have any brothers or sisters?”

“No, I’m an only child. I told them when they got me that they couldn’t do any better.”

“Wow, aren’t we stuck on our self.” Sally laughs. “He’s just kidding. He has a younger brother. Who I might add, is better looking,” They all laugh.

Jimmy comes home from work and kisses Sandy, then he hugs Sally.

“Jimmy, this is Sally’s friend Ronny.”

Jimmy shakes Ronny's hand. "Glad to meet you, Ronny. How did you and Sally meet?"

"We met in English class. I made an excuse to meet her by telling her I had lost my notes. I asked her if she would share hers. Pretty lame, but she was nice enough to share, even though she saw through my plan. She's a lot smarter than I am so her notes were better than mine anyway."

"Nice one. Ronny. I saw Sandy in the hall when I was in the fifth grade, and it took me until the seventh grade to get up the nerve to talk to her. She finally gave in and went steady with me. I think just to shut me up." They all laughed.

Ronny liked Jimmy and Sandy. "We thought if you guys wanted to, we could double date this Saturday night. Maybe a quick dinner and a movie?"

"That sounds good," Jimmy says. "I've been working so many hours; we haven't gotten to go out much. How about it, Sandy?"

"As you said, we haven't gone to a movie in forever. There is a new one at the downtown cinema. We could go to the deli next door for a quick bite. It's not real expensive, and we can save money for popcorn."

"It's a date then. We better go, Sally. Your mom and dad are expecting us for dinner. I don't want to be late. I need the brownie points."

Sally smiled at Ronnie. “I know they’re going to love you. What’s not to love? Right?”

After they leave, Sandy looks over at Jimmy. “What do you think? I like him. He has a good sense of humor, he’s cute too.”

“Don’t forget you’re a married woman now. He’s a lot different from Max, that’s for sure. Have you gotten to talk to her, just the two of you about him?”

“Just a little. She said he has been a gentleman so far. They have been going together for a couple of months. He has not made a move except to kiss her. He told her he was a little old fashion. He said they should get to know each other before they decide if they are going any further.”

“Good for him. I don’t want to see Sally get hurt again.”

“Me either. I guess time will tell. We can find out more about him and how he acts Saturday night. Now, you sit down, and I’ll get us some dinner.”

“Let me help. By the way, how did your test go today?”

“I aced it. Okay, you can set the table.”

Chapter 17

After dinner, Jimmy and Sandy are sitting on the couch, watching TV. Sandy gently runs her hand through Jimmy's hair. "Hey, what do you say we go to bed early tonight?"

"Did you have a busy day at work today? You should have told me you were tired. We don't have to watch TV."

"Who said I was tired?" He takes her hand and leads her to the bedroom.

She pushes him down on the bed and jumps on top of him. He rolls over, taking her with him. She looks up at him. "You are the love of my life. I never get tired of making love to you."

"You realize I have loved you longer. You never knew I existed until I got the nerve to talk to you. You get prettier every day. I will never quit wanting you."

"Oh, Jimmy, you are making me blush."

" I just like to look at you and know you are mine. I never thought I would be so lucky."

They lay there for a time wrapped around each other. "You're right, you did me in. I'm exhausted."

"Too tired for a piece of chocolate pie? I know it's your favorite. I got the recipe from your mom. I'll bring you a piece and a glass of milk."

"That sound so good. You talked me into it. What did I ever do to deserve you?" As she walks off, he pats her on her butt.

Chapter 18

Sally and Ronny pick Jimmy and Sandy up Saturday night for the movie. They eat at the deli, go to the movie, and stuff themselves with popcorn. After the movie, they all go back to the apartment where Jimmy and Sandy live. Ronny keeps them laughing with his stories about his drama class.

Sandy notices how Ronny looks at Sally and touches her hand. Sandy and Sally go to the kitchen to get some sodas.

"What do you think of Ronny? Isn't he great?" Sally asks.

"He seems to be crazy about you. He touches your hand and looks at you like a lost puppy. How do you feel about him? Is it getting serious?"

"I'm crazy about him, too. I hope it is. I'm just a little nervous after what happened with Max."

"Just take it slow. You said he was a little old fashioned. Just don't do anything that doesn't feel right. If he wants to and you don't, just tell him you're not ready. If he cares for you, he'll understand."

"I'm so glad I have you and Jimmy. You two are such good friends."

When they come back into the room, Ronny and Jimmy are talking about Sandy's night school. "I'm so proud of her. She works hard at school and always manages to find time to keep the house and cook for us." He looks up at Sandy. "That's my woman."

Sally sits down by Ronny, and he puts his arm around her.

"This is my woman, I hope. I'm pretty nuts about her. I hope it's going where I think it is."

She leans over and puts her head on his shoulder. "I think you're right. I'm nuts about you, too."

They sit and talk for hours. Finally, Sally says they better go and reminds them it's getting late. They say goodbye, and Sally promises to call Sandy later.

Chapter 19

Ronny opens the car door for Sally. She turns to look at him before she gets in. “I’m so glad you and Jimmy get along so well. He and Sandy are so important to me.”

“I hope I’m that important to you.” He kisses her then she gets in. They head back to Sally’s parents. “You know we have talked about moving in together, and you have never said yes.”

“I know, but it’s a big step. I mean – we – I just don’t want to get hurt.”

“Sally, I would never hurt you. I’m in love with you. I want this to go further than just in college. I want it to be a lifetime thing. I’ve never felt this way about anyone else. You’re so different from the other girls. You are waiting for the one who really is the one for you. Some of the others, well, they don’t have much respect for themselves. It doesn’t seem to matter who it is; it’s all in fun. You know what I’m trying to say, don’t you?”

“Yes, and I’m glad you feel that way about me. I’m in love with you, too. I do want to move in with you. It just took me some time to realize how I felt about you.”

Chapter 20

Ronnie and Sally returned to college. "I had a great time this weekend. It was nice to meet your parents and I liked your friends Sandy and Jimmy."

"They liked you too," said Sally. "I could tell."

When they get to Sally's apartment, he opens the car door for her. "You know it's late. I hate for you to drive all the way to your apartment when you're already here, and mine is just a few steps away." Sally looks up at him and smiles.

"Are you sure, Sally? I know we've waited for this. I just want you to be sure. I would never push you to do something you don't want to."

Sally stands up on her tiptoes and kisses him. "I'm sure, Ronny. You're the one I've been waiting for."

Inside her apartment, he takes her in his arms and kisses her a deep passionate kiss. She feels his passion and leans into him. She takes his hand and leads him to her bedroom. He picks her up and gently lays her down on the bed. He takes his shirt off and sits down beside her. "You're a beautiful woman, Sally. I have wanted to make love to you since the first day I asked you to share your English notes with me."

"I'm just a little nervous. I'm sorry."

He kisses her again. "I love you, Sally," he says.

He looks down at her, and there are tears in her eyes. "Oh, Sally, What have I done? I'm so sorry."

"I'm crying because I am so happy. I'm glad I waited for you. I never knew it could be like this. To be with someone you love and to make love is something so special. Do you think I'm silly?"

"No, I feel the same way. I never want to lose you, Sally. I mean that. I want to spend the rest of my life with you. As soon as I get my degree, will you marry me?"

"Are you sure? We haven't known each other but a few months. What if you change your mind?"

"I won't, but I'll ask you again on the day I graduate. But for now, will you say yes?"

"Yes, Yes. I'll marry you."

Chapter 21

The next morning she wakes up before he does and slips out of bed. She showers then goes to the kitchen to make coffee. The phone rings. She knows who it is before she answers. It's Sandy.

"Hello, I knew that was you before I answered. I'm glad you both liked him. I was making coffee for us."

"For us?" Sandy ask?"

"Yes, us usually means two or more. And there are two here. Ronny spent the night with me. We're going to move in together. He asked me to marry him after he gets his degree, and I said yes. I can't talk now; I hear him getting up. I'll call you later. Yes, it was wonderful. Got to go. Bye." She hangs up just as Ronny walks into the kitchen, wearing only his jeans.

"Good morning, beautiful. Do I smell coffee?" He pulls her into his arms. "Is my answer still the same this morning, or have you decided you made a mistake? I hope not. I meant what I said. I do love you." He kisses her a deep passionate kiss.

"Yes, you smell coffee. And yes, my answer is still the same. Would you like for me to fix us some breakfast? Do you have time?"

"Yes, breakfast would be great. I'm hungry."

"You know we haven't known each other for very long. It just seems like I've known you all my life."

She looks deep into his eyes and sees the love he has for her – the same love she has for him. "*You* are wonderful. I can't wait for us to move in together."

He smiles at her. I can help; I'm a pretty good cook."

Chapter 22

Sandy's phone rings. "Hello, Sally. I've been waiting to hear everything, and I'm so happy for you. He seems like a great guy."

"Well, what was it like? I remember our first time. Of course, that was in the back seat of his old Ford. Yeah, sometimes I attack him. He loves it when I do. I guess it lets him know I love him and want him as much as he wants me. I could never get tired of making love to him. Okay, talk to you later. Glad you're happy. Bye."

Jimmy comes in from the bedroom. "Was that Sally?"

"Yes, she and Ronny are moving in together. He stayed with her last night. He even asked her to marry him as soon as he gets his degree. I'm so happy for her. She finally has the right one. Just like me!"

Chapter 23

A few weeks later, Sandy is at her mom's house. "Tomorrow, I graduate from night school. I'm so excited! It's been kind of hard because I took extra classes to finish sooner. But it was worth it. Now I can apply for a job with the insurance company. I got an application last week on line. I have all the qualifications they are asking for."

"That's great, honey. Your dad and I are really proud of you. You two are doing so well. It's been a long six months, but you made it."

"I got to go, Mom. Tell Dad I love him too. Jimmy and I are going out to dinner to celebrate. I want to go home and change before we go. I bought some new jeans and a shirt." She kisses her mom and runs out the door.

Sandy rushes home. She can't wait to see Jimmy.

"You sure look pretty, Sandy. I like your new outfit. It shows off all of your curves. Are you ready to go?"

"Yes, just give me a minute to finish my hair."

"You know how proud of you I am? You worked so hard to finish your administrative management program. You'll be running the place before long."

"Let's just wait until I get the job first."

On the way home from dinner, Sandy tells Jimmy she talked to Sally today. "She and Ronny are getting very serious. They are thinking about moving in together. He has an apartment off campus, and Sally said it's nice and close enough to walk to class. I'm happy for her. She will be in town in a couple of weeks, and I thought I'd meet her for some girl time."

"That sounds like a good idea. You two don't get to spend much time together. It will be good for you to get out. Away from your grumpy husband."

"Yes, it would be good to get away from my very *sexy* grumpy husband."

"Just as long as you come back. And I like that part about sexy."

The weeks pass, and Sandy meets Sally for lunch. "I'm so glad you could drive in from college to meet me." said Sandy. "We don't get to spend much time together now that I am married and you are going to college in another town."

"You look like the cat that ate the canary. What's going on Sally?"

"First, I've moved in with Ronny, and second, I've never been so happy."

"Sally, I'm so happy for you. I can't wait to tell Jimmy. He is going to be happy for you, too."

After lunch, Sandy leaves the cafe and pulls out into the intersection. Just as she starts to turn, a car runs the stop sign and slams into her side of the car. Her car spins around and comes to a stop against a light pole. The other car flips over and lands on its side. People rush out to see if they can help. Someone dials 911. In a few minutes, the emergency vehicles arrive. Sandy is taken to the hospital, as is the driver of the other car.

Chapter 24

An officer appears at Jimmy's work and tells him that Sandy has been in an accident. Mel takes Jimmy to the hospital as he is too shaken up to drive. Mel calls Sandy's parents and Jimmy's parents. He's in the waiting room with Jimmy when they arrive.

"What happened? How is Sandy?" Her mother and dad are frantic.

"I don't know. They haven't told me anything yet. She's in surgery."

Jimmy's dad puts his arm around him, and his mom moves in close to her son's other side.

A long time passes, and finally, the doctor comes in. "Mr. Johnson, I'm sorry. We did all we could. Her internal injuries were too severe."

"No! No! You're wrong! I want to see her." His dad holds him, as Jimmy tries to break away. "No!" He crumbles to the floor. "She can't be gone; she's got to be okay."

His dad kneels and holds him. His mother manages to get to a chair. Sandy's mother is crying hysterically, and her husband is holding her and crying also.

Jimmy stops crying and looks up at the doctor. "I want to see her."

“It will be a few minutes. The nurse will come and get you.”

Jimmy gets to his feet and goes over to Sandy’s parents. The three of them hold each other. “I can’t live without her; she’s my whole world. I don’t *want* to live without her. Why did this happen? We were supposed to spend the rest of our lives together.” He sees a nurse coming toward them.

“Harry and Judy, do you want to come with me?” He looks at her parents.

“Go ahead, son. We will wait and give you some time with her.”

Jimmy walks off in a daze.

Chapter 25

On the day of Sandy's funeral, Jimmy is at home sitting in his chair. Someone knocks at the door. He ignores it. They knock again. He still ignores it. The door opens, and his mother and dad come in.

"Jimmy, you're not dressed. The funeral is in an hour. We need to be going to the church." His mother is kneeling in front of him.

"I'm not going."

"What do you mean, you're not going? You need to say goodbye to Sandy."

"Come on, Jimmy. I will help you get your things." His dad says.

"What don't you understand? I'm not going!"

"Why don't you want to go? I know this is hard, but you need to say goodbye to her."

"I'm not going because if I go, it means she's really gone." He breaks down and puts his head in his hands.

His dad sits down on the chair in front of him. "Jimmy, you know we loved Sandy, too. But it wouldn't be right not to go and be there for her."

"She's not there. Don't you see? I'm lost without her. If I go, then I'll have to come home without her. I can't do it."

"Yes, you can, and you will. You have to be strong. She wouldn't want you to feel this way. She loved you and would want you to go on with your life. You need to honor her by doing that."

Jimmy looks up at him. "I don't know if I can, but for her, I'll try."

Chapter 26

After the funeral, Jimmy has had enough of all of the people and their sorrowful faces. He leaves out the side door. His next stop is a bar downtown, where he spends the rest of the day. At closing time, they ask him to leave. He staggers out to his car and gets in. The bartender sees that he is going to drive and approaches his window.

“Hey buddy, you don’t need to be driving. Let me call you a cab.” He is talking to himself. Jimmy has passed out with his head against the steering wheel. He steps back inside and calls the police.

“Where am I?” Jimmy sits up and looks around. He sees he is in jail.

“Hey! You! Why am I here?”

The officer standing there looks at him. “You were drunk, and you fought the officer when he tried to talk to you. You got somebody to call? I can let you make a phone call if you like.”

Jimmy makes his call. “Dad, I need you to come and get me. No, I’m in jail. I guess I drank too much, and I don’t remember what happened after that.”

Mr. Johnson is waiting when Jimmy is brought out. “Are you okay?” he asks his son.

"I guess so. Thanks for getting me out. I just want to go home." Jimmy sits in silence on the way home. "I would rather be by myself. You go on home, Dad. I'll be okay. I'll call you later."

When Stan gets home, his wife Nancy is waiting by the front door. "Is he all right? What did he do to get put in jail?"

"He got drunk and got into it with an officer who tried to help him. I'm worried about him. I have never known him to drink more than one beer. I didn't see him leave the funeral yesterday. He doesn't know what to do without Sandy."

"It will take some time, Stan. He is still in shock. We just need to stay close to him. Sandy was his everything, since they were in school. We just need to be there for him."

Chapter 27

Six weeks later, Jimmy has still not gone back to work. He is still in the same clothes he put on two days ago. He doesn't answer the phone.

His boss Mel knocks, but he doesn't answer. Mel tries the door, and it's unlocked. "Jimmy, are you in there?" He walks in and sees Jimmy sitting on the couch. "I've been trying to reach you. I've been calling you. I'm worried about you."

"Don't worry about me. I'm okay. I just want to be left alone. You need to find someone else to work for you. I'm not coming back. I don't know what I'm going to do. I don't mean to rude. I just want to be left alone."

"I know it's going to take some time, but you will need to work. I'll keep your job open for you. I want you back. You're good at your job, and it's hard to find someone as good as you."

"Please just get someone else. I don't want to come back. I just want to be left alone."

"Okay, but I'm still going to wait for another three weeks. Let me know if you change your mind." He stops at the door and looks back at Jimmy. "Take care of yourself."

Later that night, his mother and dad come by. They knock and yell through the door. "Jimmy, it's Mom and Dad. Can we come in?"

Jimmy gets up and opens the door. "Hi," he mutters, then turns and walks back to the couch.

"Your mother made you some dinner. I know you need some time son, but she's worried you're not eating." His mother puts the tray of food in front of him on the coffee table. "I made your favorites. I brought you a piece of chocolate cake too." They both sit down in the chairs opposite Jimmy.

"Thanks, Mom. I guess I don't think about eating. I don't think about much of anything but Sandy. I keep wanting for her to walk through the door. But she isn't going to, she's gone." He puts his head in his hands and looks down at the floor.

His dad goes over to the couch and puts his arm around him. Jimmy breaks down and puts his head against his dad's shoulder. "Jimmy, you need to go on with your life. Sandy wouldn't want you to just give up. She loved you too much; she wouldn't want to see you this way. You had a very special love. Just think of all the good times you had together. Be grateful for that special love. Some people never get to have that. Keep your memories in your heart. You need to honor her love by going on with your life. By doing something good with your life. Help other people, give your time to something good. She loved animals, do something with them."

Jimmy looked up at his dad. “I don’t know what that would be. I don’t know how to do anything but be a mechanic.”

“Just think about it. We love you, son. Will you call us if you need anything?”

“Yes, Dad. I’ll try to think of something. Please don’t worry. Just give me some time.”

Chapter 28

Another two weeks go by with Jimmy trying to decide what he wants to do with the rest of his life. He thinks about what his dad said about Sandy loving animals. He's watching TV and sees a documentary about dogs in the service. He hasn't ever thought about enlisting. He watches the whole thing. *I wonder if I could enlist and learn to work with dogs. They do a lot of good things. I could do something for my country and do something Sandy would be proud of me for. She did love dogs.* He picks up his cell and calls the number on the screen to find an office near to him. He makes an appointment for the next day. He goes to bed and sleeps for the first time. He feels like he has a new goal in life. He feels Sandy would approve.

The next morning, he is at the Marine recruiting office. He sits down with a sergeant who is in charge of recruitment. "Why do you want to enlist, son?"

"I recently lost my wife. I need to have a fresh start, and I want to do something with my life. I would really like to work with the canine unit. I love dogs and I'm good with them. Is that a possibility?"

"Have you really given this a lot of thought? If you enlist it would be for a few years. There is a good chance you could be in the canine unit. You would have to go through boot camp first, and advanced Infantry training, then you could put in for canine training. I can put that on your recruitment papers. That would help them to see what you want to do. Are you physically okay?"

"Yes, I'm in good shape. I don't wear glasses; I have excellent vision. I would really like to enlist."

"Okay, Let's fill out the papers and get things started."

Jimmy left the recruitment office and felt good, he had a purpose. He would be back to take his physical in a couple of days. He went to see his parents to tell them what he was going to do.

Chapter 29

When he arrived, his mother and dad were in the living room. He sat down opposite them. "I need to tell you something, and I'm not sure you will approve, but it's what I want to do. I've enlisted in the Marines. I want to be in their canine unit. I will have to go through regular training, and then there is a chance I can train to be in the canine unit."

His mother and dad both spoke at once. "Why do you have to do that? Can't you find something here to do? They might send you overseas. There is a lot of fighting going on and you might get right in the middle of it. Please reconsider."

"Please understand, I need to do this. It gives me a purpose. I have to find something that gives me a reason to go from one day to the next. I'm sure of this."

"I guess if this is what you want, son." His father gets up, and Jimmy gets up too. He hugs him, and his mother finally comes over to them and hugs both of them. His mother tries not to cry, but the tears roll down her cheeks.

"It's okay, Mom I'll be okay."

Jimmy takes his physical and is told to be at the office in two days to leave for boot camp. He finds someone to take over his apartment and puts his things in storage. As he leaves the apartment for the last time, he turns and says, “Well, my love, I guess we’re in the Marines now.”

Chapter 30

Jimmy arrives at boot camp and is shown his bunk. He stores his stuff and meets another soldier who bunks in the same barracks.

"Hey, my name is Jerry. I got here this morning. You just get here?"

"Yeah, my name is Jimmy. I guess we start training first thing in the morning."

"You from around here?"

"No, I'm from Texas. You?"

"I'm from Oklahoma. Pretty close, huh."

"Yeah, I got into some trouble, and my old man said I needed something to do other than stay in trouble. He took me down to the enlistment office.

"How about you?"

"I just decided to join. Think I'll look around." He turns and walks outside.

Chapter 31

The next morning they are rousted out of bed by reveille. “Everyone fall in” He takes them to one of the buildings. “Get in line and get your uniforms. Then you’re going to get a haircut.” After all of the men are dressed, he takes them to another one of the buildings. “You’re getting a High and Tight. That long hair is gone.” In just a few minutes they are almost bald. “You look great ladies. Outside,” the sergeant says. “Okay, fall in and step into those yellow footsteps.”

They fall into place and are yelled at first thing.

“You are in the Marines now. You will be worked hard, and you will be given orders. You will follow those orders no matter what they are. You will not deviate from those orders. You will be trained to be the best Marine you can be. Do you understand?”

“Yes, Sir!” is the cry in unison.

“I DIDN’T HEAR YOU!”

“YES, SIR!” The cry is louder.

“Fall in and follow me.”

They were drilled harder and harder until they could barely stand. When the first day was over they fell into their bunks, only to repeat the same day after day for 12 weeks.

Chapter 32

One day after training they were all standing around when one of the Sergeant came up and ask for private Phillips. Their Sergeant yelled. "Private Phillips step forward." He came running and stopped in front of the Sergeant. The first Sergeant said you won't be seeing him anymore, and led him off. We all wondered what was going on. Later we found out he was only fourteen years old. He had lied about his age and forged his Mothers signature. She had found out from one of his buddies that he had joined the Marines.

Dear Mom and Dad,

We go from sunup to sundown. I'm getting in pretty good shape. I've got muscles I didn't know I had. I've got aches I never had, either .How are you doing? Do you ever see Sandy's parents? Are they doing okay? I know it was hard on them, losing their only child. I couldn't bring myself to say goodbye to them. If you see them, tell them I'm sorry.

Boot camp is finally over, and now I go to advanced infantry training.

Not much to tell you. I'll see you when training camp is over. I have not heard about the canine unit yet. Hope to hear something when I return.

I get a one-week leave.

Love to you both,

Jimmy

Weeks go by, and the training camp finally comes to an end. He had not heard about joining the canine unit. Instead, he is assigned to the rifle unit. Jimmy writes to his parents and tells them he is coming home for a week.

He isn't sure where he is going to be stationed. He says goodbye to Jerry. They have grown to be good friends. They both go home for leave.

Chapter 33

"You look good, Son. I'm glad you're home. Your mother will be down in a minute. She didn't hear you come in. Are you doing okay? Have you heard where you're going to be stationed?"

"It's good to be home, Dad. No, they said we would get our orders when we get back to camp."

"Jimmy! I didn't hear you come in." His mom hugs him and holds on. "I've missed you so much. Your room is ready for you. What would you like for dinner? I'll fix your favorites."

"Nancy, let the boy breathe. He just got here."

"I'm so glad you're home. Do you really think they will send you overseas? You have only had a few weeks of training."

"I don't know, Mom. Have you talked to Sandy's parents? I thought I'd go see them while I'm home. What do you think?"

"I think they would love to see you. They always ask about you. You were like a son to them. They know how much you and Sandy loved each other."

"I will go see them in a few days. I just want to spend time with you and Dad."

“Sally called to ask about you. She missed you at the funeral. You should give her a call, too.”

“Yeah, I need to call her. I owe her an apology. I saw her at the funeral, but I just couldn’t talk to anyone. That’s why I left.”

“Don’t feel bad; everyone understood. I’m sure Sally did. She was so close to Sandy, like a sister. She came by before she went back to college. She’s a really nice girl.”

Chapter 34

The next morning Jimmy calls Sally and makes arrangements to see her in a couple of days. He spends the rest of the day with his parents. He goes to see Sandy's parents the following day. Tomorrow was the day to meet Sally. He dreads it. It would bring back so many memories. But he owes her for leaving and not saying goodbye.

They meet at a restaurant downtown. They get a booth and order something to drink. "Tell me about you and Ronny. How is it going?"

"It's going great. He is wonderful and treats me so good. He does all the little things that let me know he loves me. He has another year to finish his degree, then we're going to get married."

"I'm really happy for you, Sally. You found the right one. I hope you're as happy as Sandy and I were." He looks away so she won't see the tears.

"I know how much you loved each other. I miss her so much. It was like losing a sister. Tell me what you're doing now. I went by the garage, and Mel said you weren't working there anymore."

"I joined the Marines. I am home on leave. I want to work with the canine unit. I'm hoping to get a chance. I'm in the rifle unit now." They have lunch and talk for a couple of hours. She has to leave to go back to school, so they say goodbye.

"Take care of yourself," she says as they step outside.

"Okay, I will. Be happy, Sally. Sandy always said you would find the same thing she and I had. I'm glad you did."

Chapter 35

Jimmy calls Sandy's parents and asks if he could stop by. They say they would love to see him, for him to come right over.

Mrs. Taylor opens the door and hugs Jimmy. "We're so glad you came to see us. We didn't get to see you before you left. Your mom told me you had joined the Marines. She said you wanted to work with the canine unit. I think that is wonderful. Oh, I'm sorry. Come in. Harry is in the den. Can I get you something to drink?"

"No thanks, I just had lunch. Hello, Mr. Taylor." He sticks out his hand to shake Mr. Taylor's hand. "I owe you both an apology. I didn't talk to you at the funeral. I left and didn't talk to anyone. I just couldn't. I'm sorry."

"It's okay, son. We understood. Sit down and tell us about your Marines."

"Not much to tell. The training was tough. I'm not sure where they're going to send me I won't know until I get back to camp. They are sending some men overseas, so I guess there is a possibility that's where I'll go. I'm still hoping to get to work with the canine unit. They have put me in the rifle unit for now."

They talk for a couple of hours, and he tells them he is expected home for dinner and he needs to leave. As he starts out the front door,

Mrs. Taylor hugs him. "Take care of yourself, Jimmy. You know we both love you." He sees tears in her eyes.

"I will, and thank you."

On the last day of his leave, he sits with his mom and dad in the den. His mom is trying not to cry, but the tears are there no matter how hard she tries to hold them back. "Write to us as often as you can so we'll know you're okay. If you can tell us where you're going to be stationed, I can write to you."

"Okay, Mom. I'll try. I guess I better get my gear together. I'm supposed to be at the bus station at five." He gets up and goes upstairs to get his things. When he comes back down, his dad asks if he wants him to drive him to the station. "No thanks, Dad. I'd rather you stay here with Mom." He kisses them goodbye and heads out to the cab that has just driven up. His parents stand at the door and watch until the cab is out of sight.

Chapter 36

Jimmy gets back to the base late and hits the bunk. Early comes early in the Marines. Sure enough, it seems like he has just closed his eyes when reveille calls. He hits the floor and is out the door in a matter of minutes. They all fall in to await their orders. The sergeant starts yelling out to each man his orders and where he is going to be sent. Jimmy is waiting to hear if he is still going to be in the rifle unit or not. Everyone has been called but him.

"Johnson, step forward."

"Yes, Sir."

"You had put in a request for the canine unit. You have been assigned to the rifle unit, but there is an opening in the canine unit if you are still interested."

"Yes, sir. I would still like to be assigned to the canine unit, sir."

"Very well. You will report to Sergeant Nelson in the division headquarters for further orders. Dismissed."

Jimmy can't believe he is actually getting to work with the canine unit. He has always admired the men who worked and trained with them. He had seen pictures of them in the line of fire with their dogs, either doing a bomb search or going after the enemy.

Two days later, he was to start training on how to handle a dog. It was going to be a long process to learn everything. He and the dog had to work as one, and know what the other was going to do in any situation. He worked with a dog that was already trained before he was given a dog that was going to be his partner. He spent six weeks with an instructor and the dogs.

He was finally given a German shepherd named Hero. Hero had been in combat with his handler, who had been wounded and sent home. Now Hero was to be his. He and Hero were together constantly. Training together and sleeping together. This was important for them to learn about each other before going in to battle. They grew to have great respect for each other. They had to depend on each other. Their lives would depend on the trust they had for each other. Finally, the day came when they were going to be deployed overseas.

They were helicoptered to a base not far from the front line. They were sent on several missions. Hero and Jimmy worked as one, a team, a partnership. Jimmy was always aware of not only his safety but of Hero's also. He and some of the other men got to be friends. Every now and then, they had some time when they could relax. Jimmy learned to play poker – no, he learned to *lose* at poker. No matter where he was, Hero was always by his side.

Chapter 37

On one of the missions, his unit was pinned down under fire. He and Hero had to reach the men who had the machine guns. They were at the top of the hill and had better cover than his unit. He and Hero circled around behind them and Hero took care of one of them while Jimmy took out the other one. He signaled for his unit and they continued their raid on the enemy. They only had one casualty. One of the men stepped on a land mine. He was killed instantly. When they made it back to camp. Jimmy realized Hero was limping. He bandaged his leg to give it support. All the men said Hero was a Hero, and Jimmy wasn't bad either.

Hero was given a few days to let his leg heal before they were sent out again. Each time he and Jimmy worked better than the time before. They had been in combat for about six months before all hell broke loose. The unit was to rescue a couple of army guys who had been captured. This was deep in enemy territory. They were able to get into the camp where the two men were being held but were out-numbered. The fight lasted for hours. Finally, they made a break and got out with the two men. As they were getting away, they came under fire from another direction, and some of his men were hit. Jimmy and Hero went after a man who was down and taking fire, and dragged him to cover. Jimmy was hit in the leg. He looked down and Hero had been hit in the shoulder. His unit was heading back to camp, carrying the wounded. Jimmy put Hero around his neck and carried him back.

"You're going to be okay, Hero. We're almost there. I've got you; you're going to be okay." Jimmy took him to the tent where the medic was. He wouldn't let them check his leg until they had taken care of Hero. "Is he going to be okay, Doc? He's got to be okay. He's my buddy. Hero, it's me. Hang in there, boy, the doc is going to take care of you."

"He's going to have to be sent back to be taken care of. I can't do what needs to be done here. I can patch you up, but you'll have to go with him too."

"You're right about that, I'm not leaving him."

Chapter 38

Hero and Jimmy were air-lifted back to the base hospital. Jimmy stayed by Hero's side until they kicked him out of the operating room. It was pretty bad. The bullet had done some damage, but it could be repaired.

Jimmy called his parents to tell them what happened. He told them not to worry, he was going to be okay. He had to have some surgery on his leg, then he would have to go to rehab. He told them he would be sent to the VA hospital near them but would have to stay at the hospital for a while. He explained what had happened to Hero and said he was going to see if he could adopt him because Hero was going to be discharged, too. His wound was so bad he couldn't be sent back into battle.

Dad, "I know this is a lot to ask, but since I can't keep Hero with me until I am released, could you and Mom keep him for me until I get to come home? He means so much to me. He's not just my partner, he's my best friend. I can't let him be sent to someone who will not love and take care of him like I would."

"Of course we will Jimmy. Just tell us what we have to do and where we go to get him. We will take good care of him until you get home. I know how much he means to you. Don't worry about him, just take care of yourself. Let us know when you will be at the VA. We can come to see you, and maybe they will let Hero visit you too."

"Thank you so much, Dad, and thank Mom too. You will love him. He's such a great dog. He is almost human. He understands everything you say to him. If you have anything of mine you can put it in his bed and he will know I'm going to be coming after him.

Chapter 39

Jimmy's surgery was very extensive. He had been hit in the upper part of his leg, and it had done a lot of damage. He had not realized how bad it was. He had been too worried about Hero.

The next morning after surgery, when Jimmy wakes up, he asks about Hero the first thing.

"He's doing great. He will be glad to see you. You can't get up yet. You need to give your leg some time to heal. You had a lot of damage that had to be repaired. It was worse than we thought. You're lucky you didn't lose your leg. You'll have to be in a wheelchair for a time. You're going to have to have some therapy before you can use your leg again. Hero still has to be kept quiet, too, for another two or three days. So just relax – you're not going anywhere."

Three days later, Jimmy stood it as long as he could. He managed to get into the wheelchair beside his bed and was on his way to see Hero.

"Hi, boy. I missed you. Are you okay? We both had a bad day, didn't we? But we're going to be okay now. The doc says you're going to be okay."

Hero is laying down, but his tail is wagging. Jimmy's chair is down where he is on eye level with Hero. He strokes his head and leans over for a big lick on the face. “That’s my guy,” Jimmy says.

Chapter 40

The doctor comes in and has some papers in his hand. "I'm afraid Hero has seen his last battle. His injury has made it impossible for him to return to duty. He will be sent home. And what are you doing out of bed? You're not supposed to be moving around much."

"I had to see Hero and see if he was going to be okay. I kind of snuck out."

Jimmy looks at Hero. "Well, Hero, it looks like we're in the same boat. I'm being sent home too. I'm going to do everything in my power to get you assigned to me. My leg will never be the same. You and I are a pair. I'll be back later; I've got some papers I need to file so I can take you home with me."

"Don't worry about Hero, I'll take care of him until you get back."

"Thanks, Doc. I don't know what I need to do, but I'm going to do it." He turns his wheelchair and he's out the door, heading for his commander's office.

Chapter 41

"I'm sorry Jimmy, that's not the way it works. He will be sent back to the training school, and then they will find him a home. You will be sent back to a VA hospital to do rehab. It will be some time before you can go home. He can't stay with you at rehab."

"What if I get someone in my family to keep him for me until I'm able to go home. Can I petition for him as guardianship?"

"I don't know, I guess it can be done. Let me check on it for you. Give me a couple of days to find out what I can."

"When Is Hero being sent back to his training camp?"

"I'm not sure, I'll find out. He still has some recovery to do before he can be signed out."

"I'll wait for you to get in touch with me. I'm going back to see him. I don't leave for the states for a few more days. Please do whatever you can for me and Hero. He saved a lot of lives, and he deserves to go to someone who was there with him."

"I'll do my best soldier. I know how close you guys work with your canine partners.

Chapter 42

Jimmy is on his way to see Hero when he hears a familiar voice. “Jimmy, wait up.”

“Conrad, how are you doing. I didn’t know you were here.”

“I finally got them to let me out of the hospital. My arm is going to be okay. Thanks to you and Hero. If you had not pulled me to safety I would have been dead meat. When I went down it knocked the breath out of me. I couldn’t move. I owe you two my life. Where is Hero anyway?”

“He’s in the hospital too. He took a hit in the shoulder. It was pretty bad. He is going to be sent back. I’m trying to get him released to me. But there is a lot of paper work to do first. The Sarge is working on it for me. I’ve got to go to rehab and he can’t stay in rehab with me. I going to try to get him sent to my parents' house until I get home.”

“If I can do anything to help just let me know. I can talk to Sarge for you. Maybe that would help.”

“Thanks man, I would really appreciate it. Anything will help.”

“Okay, I’ll go see him now. I will come by the hospital later and let you know how it goes.”

“How did it go about Hero?” The doctor asks.

“Not sure, you know how red tape is. I’ll just have to wait and see. I’m going in to see Hero and tell him what’s going on.”

Chapter 43

Three days passed and Jimmy had not heard anything back about Hero and he was about to be sent to the VA hospital for rehab. He was on his way to see the Sergeant when the Sergeant ran into him.

"I was looking for you, Jimmy. Hero is going to have to go back to his training camp, but I filed a request for him to be held until your parents could make arrangements to go and get him."

"That's great. Thanks, Sarge. I'll call my dad and he can make all the arrangements. I've got to go tell Hero."

"Wait! I haven't given you the number to call, and you have to come to my office and sign the papers for his transfer."

"Oh, I was so excited I didn't think. I'll follow you back to your office." Jimmy wheeled around in his chair and followed Sarge back to his office.

After the papers are all taken care of Jimmy goes to tell Hero he is going home. Hero is sitting up when Jimmy comes in. "Hey Hero, you're looking good. How is everything, doc?"

"He is recovering nicely. His wounds will take a while to heal. He is going to have to wear that bandage and brace for a couple of weeks at least. Then he will have to be looked at by a veterinary hospital."

"My mom and dad are going to go and get him at his training camp. He is going to be mine forever. They will take care of him until I get out of rehab." He reaches out and pets Hero. You're going home Hero. You'll love my mom and dad, and they will take good care of you until I get home. Look, Doc. He understands. Look at his tail wag."

Chapter 44

Jimmy is packing to go to the VA hospital when his sergeant says he has to delay his trip. He is to report to the canine hospital. Jimmy is terrified. He is afraid something has happened to Hero. When he arrives, he finds Hero sitting beside one of the sergeants he had had in training.

Jimmy salutes the sergeant and asks what is going on. The sergeant stands and brings Hero over beside Jimmy. Another soldier brings three small boxes forward and hands one of them to the sergeant.

"It is my honor to present you with the Purple Heart for being wounded while serving. You and Hero risked your lives to pull a wounded soldier to cover under fire." He pins the Medal to Jimmy's uniform. "It is also my honor to present Hero with the Purple Heart for being wounded while serving." He hands the Purple Heart for Hero to Jimmy. It is attached to a collar. Jimmy reaches down from his wheelchair and places it around Hero's neck. "It is also my honor to present you with the Bronze Star for Valor." He pins the other medal on Jimmy's uniform beside the earlier medal he had received. He backs up and salutes both Jimmy and Hero. Jimmy salutes him back.

"Thank you Sir. And thank you from Hero.

The sergeant bends down, and Hero raises his paw to shake his hand. "We're very proud of you too Hero."

Jimmy has tears in his eyes and wipes them away when no one is looking. "I don't deserve this medal more than the other men who fought beside us. They are all brave men who would die for their country. I am honored, Sir, and very proud to be a Marine."

The next morning Jimmy and Hero are put on a Hospital plane and sent to their separate destinations.

Chapter 45

While eating breakfast one morning, Nancy remarks to her husband Stan, "I'm so excited we get to keep Hero for Jimmy. He really loves that dog."

"Yeah, they worked together for over six months. He actually carried him back to their camp when he got shot. I'm so proud of Jimmy. He seems to be getting his life back on track after losing Sandy."

Stan answered back. "I was worried about him. He was so depressed. I think the Marines and Hero were good for him. I know he's facing a long battle with his leg. I'm just glad he didn't lose it because of his injuries. And if he had lost Hero, it would have been like losing his best friend. I don't know how he would have handled another loss. I'm just glad he got to keep Hero. I think he gave Jimmy a reason to hurry and get through rehab. He said in one of his letters how hard it was to lose one of the guys in his unit. He has had a lot of hardships in his life already."

"He will have something to look forward to when he gets out of the VA," Nancy said. "I'm sure Hero will be glad to see him too. I did what Jimmy said and got one of his old sweat shirts and put it in the bed we bought for Hero. Even though it's been washed, it might still have some of Jimmy's smell. I also brought one with me to show Hero we're his new grandparents, and he is going to stay with us until Jimmy gets home. I know dogs have such a keen sense of smell. Even things we can't smell, they can. I just hope he's happy with us until Jimmy gets home."

Chapter 46

"I hope they let us take Hero into the rehab hospital," said Jimmy's mom. "Since Hero is a hero and a veteran also, they might," replied his dad. Jimmy's mom continued, "Especially since, along with Jimmy, the dog earned a Purple Heart for helping save another Marine. Besides that Jimmy is his best friend and it will cheer him up. That's what I'm going to tell them when we go. I'm taking Hero with us and they better not try to keep him out."

"Wow, you never cease to surprise me Nancy. Tell me how you really feel."

"Ha,Ha, you're very funny. Mothers can get away with things, especially if their defending their children."

"I wouldn't exactly call Jimmy a child, or were you talking about Hero?"

"Both, I guess. How long before we get there?"

"Not long, just about fifteen minutes. There is the sigh up ahead for our turn off."

They park the car and are trying to figure out which building it is. A woman asks if they need any help.

"Yes, thank you. My name is Stan Johnson and this is my wife Nancy Johnson. We're here to pick up a dog for my son, Jimmy, who was wounded. He was Hero's handler. I'm not sure where we should go."

"Hello, my name is Linda. I was just on my way to the administration building. That's most likely where you should try first. You can follow me if you like."

"Thank you. We're really excited. His name is Hero. He received a Purple Heart for helping our son, Jimmy to save a marine. He is going to stay with us until our son gets to come home. Jimmy has to stay at the Veteran's hospital for rehab. We're really proud of our son, he not only received a Purple Heart, but the Bronze Star for Valor."

"I don't blame you Mrs. Johnson. You should be proud of him. I'm glad you get to keep Hero for him too. That will be a great welcome home for him to get to have Hero for good."

Linda takes them to the desk and tells the receptionist why they are there. "She will take care of you. Good luck with your new member of your family."

Mr. and Mrs. Johnson shake Linda's hand. "Thank you for your help."

Chapter 47

After filling out lots of paper work, they are taken to where the dogs are kept. They are amazed at how nice the cages are. They have very nice beds, a gate to go outside, and even music is playing softly. Their bowls are full of water and they have automatic feeding bowls. "This is so nice, and clean." Mrs. Johnson says. "They take good care of them. Hero will probably want to sleep on Jimmy's bed. Or maybe in our room, if he's lonely. I hope he likes us."

"I'm sure he will. He will get the royal treatment. This must be him."

"Mr. and Mrs. Johnson, this is Hero." She has Hero on a leash, and the collar has his Purple Heart on it. "I'm so glad you are getting him. He's a great dog. He served his country and deserves to be with his handler. Hero, shake hands with the Johnsons." Hero is sitting down and raises his paw. Both Mr. and Mrs. Johnson shake his hand.

Jimmy's mom kneels down and looks Hero in the eye. "You took care of our son, Hero, now we're going to take care of you." She reaches in her purse and pulls out the sweatshirt that had belonged to Jimmy and places it on the floor in front of Hero. He looks at her and then down at the sweatshirt and smells it. He lays down and puts his head on it. “I think he knows that belonged to our son. I hope it will make him feel better to know we have a connection to Jimmy.” She strokes his head gently and he licks her hand. When she raises up, he gets up too with the sweatshirt in his mouth.

“Well, I think he knows a Mother and Grandmother when he sees one. Are you ready to go home Hero?”

The lady hands the leash to Mr. Johnson and Hero goes to sit beside him. “I guess that’s my answer.”

They leave the training camp with Hero sitting in the back seat with his head out the window.

Mr. Johnson looks in the rear-view morrow. “It’s kind of like we have a part of Jimmy going home with us.” Then he reaches over and takes his wife’s hand and smiles.

Chapter 48

Jimmy is met at the airfield with a van to take him to the Veteran's hospital. They load him and his wheelchair and leave for the hospital. The driver tells Jimmy he was in the Navy and got wounded when their ship was hit by an enemy plane. He asks Jimmy about his injury. Jimmy tells him what happened and tells him about Hero.

The driver says, "I sure hope I get to meet Hero. He sounds like a great dog."

"He's the best," Jimmy says.

When they arrive at the Veteran's hospital, there are a lot of people waiting to help him get in and settled. He is in the room with three other soldiers who have been wounded in action. One has lost an eye and was burnt by an explosion. One lost his leg when he stepped on a land mine. The last one had an injury to his arm. He had been there for about a month and was going home the next day.

Jimmy said hello to them and felt lucky to just have the injuries he had. It was almost time for dinner, and Jimmy was glad. He hadn't eaten since breakfast and he was starving. He followed the other guys down to eat. When he saw how many others had been wounded, he was hurt for them and their families. All of these men and women had given so much for their country. Some would recover, and some would never be able to lead a normal life.

After he had gotten back to his room, a doctor stopped by to meet him. "Hello, Jimmy. My name is Dr. Nelson, and I am head of Physical Therapy here at the Veteran's hospital. I will oversee your recovery. You will work with several people who will work on different parts of your body. You need to report to the PT room by 0800 to get started. We will start your physical therapy on your leg tomorrow. Today, you will start off with some simple exercises to build up the strength in your hands and arms to propel your wheelchair until your leg heals properly. For today, just take it easy. It won't be easy from now on."

At 0800 the next morning, Jimmy was in his wheelchair at the door to the Physical Therapy room. There was a lot going on. The room was busy from one side to the other. He saw Dr. Nelson talking to another marine who was on a walking machine. He had lost part of his leg and was learning to use a prosthetic. There were other Physical Therapist helping other soldiers.

He wheeled over to Dr. Nelson who turned to say hello to him. "I'll be with you in a minute. Go over to the weights and grab some 2-pound hand weights."

Jimmy found the weights and picked up two.

"Okay," Dr. Nelson said as he walked up to Jimmy. "Start by lowering them to your side and bringing them up to your chest. Do about 10 of them and I'll send someone over to get you started on the rest. We will take it slow. You don't want to push yourself to hard. It's best to go at a steady rate."

"Yes Sir. I want to get well so I can go home. I'll do whatever you say."

Chapter 49

The Doc walked off and met two other Physical Therapists and pointed to Jimmy. One of them turned and looked at him. It was a woman – no, a girl – it was hard to tell. She was about five foot five, and it was all in the right places. She had red hair that was pulled back in a pony tail. He couldn't see what color her eyes were from that distance, but he hoped he got a closer look.

"What am I thinking? I don't want to get involved with anyone. It just gets you hurt. Sandy is the love of my life. I don't need anyone else. If she comes over to help me I'm going to tell her to get someone else. I'm sorry, Sandy. I just wasn't thinking. Your love was, is, and will always be all I need. I will never love anyone else."

Dr. Nelson brought the young woman over to introduce her to Jimmy. "Jimmy, this is Fredda. She is going to be your PT instructor. She is very good; she has been here for four years."

Jimmy said hello, then asked Dr. Nelson if he could talk to him in private. "What's wrong, Jimmy?"

"I'd rather have a man help me if it's okay. I'm sure she is good, but I'd rather have a man instructor."

“Okay, Jimmy, she is one of the best ones we have. But is you don’t feel comfortable with her, I’ll get someone else.”

“Fredda, I am going to change things up. You will help Sergeant Jacobs instead.”

Fredda looked at Jimmy and smiled. “Did I do something wrong? I actually haven’t done anything yet. So what’s your problem?”

Jimmy was surprised at her reaction. “I just want a man to help me. Okay?”

Chapter 50

He sat there for a few minutes before a big man who said his name was Mike came over to talk to him and get him started off on some exercises. He worked hard all day and before he knew it the day was almost over. He ate a big dinner. He had worked up quite an appetite. Later he went into the library to find something to read. Fredda was sitting at a table talking to another woman.

"Well, I think I'll take my book and go to another room. This room just got too crowded." She turned and looked at Jimmy than picked up her book and walked right past him. "Excuse me," she said with a sarcastic tone. He watched her walk out and didn't understand what her problem was. He really didn't care.

Jimmy was on his way to his room, and as he rounded the corner he ran into Fredda and almost knocked her down.

"Watch where you're going!" she said. "There are other people around here besides you." She picked up the books she had dropped and stormed off.

"Wow," he whispered to himself. "She has an attitude. I'm glad I got someone else to help me."

A couple of weeks went by. Jimmy worked really hard. He thought, *the sooner I get out of this chair, the sooner I can go home.* On the weekend after he had been there a month, his parents got to come and visit. They brought Hero.

Chapter 51

"I'm so glad to see you both. And you got to bring Hero. How has he been?" Hero was on his hind feet with his two front feet in Jimmy's lap. Jimmy could hardly talk for all of the licking going on.

Jimmy's mother responds "He's great. He settled in with no problem at all. He sleeps in your bed and carries your old sweatshirt around with him all the time. We had to hide it this morning, or he would have brought it with him. He is very protective of us. We have had to tell all of our friends to be careful when they first come over until he sees they are good people and not a threat to us."

"Your dad takes him for walks to the park almost every day. Or maybe Hero takes your dad to the park every day. He said so many people know now who he is and just want to either pet him or take his picture. I think Hero likes all the attention and likes to have his picture taken."

"Just be careful. Someone might want to steal him away from you. He might be worth a lot of money to someone. He is worth everything to me, just for who he is. Aren't you, boy?" Jimmy hugs Hero, and Hero's tail is going as fast as it can. "Have you seen Sandy's parents lately?"

"Yes, we have gotten to where we have dinner with them about every other week. They have also fallen in love with Hero. They always ask about you too. Sometime when you get a chance, you should write to them. You have been good about writing to us, but I think they feel close to you. You are their last connection to Sandy."

"I'll try. I just don't know what to say to them."

In between kisses from Hero, they get to talk.

"How is your physical training going? You look like you're getting some muscles. What does the doctor say about your leg?" asks Jimmy's dad.

"I am getting some upper-body strength. I will be starting to work on my legs in a few weeks. It's just going to take some time. Dr. Nelson said to take it slow and build up a little at a time."

Jimmy took his parents to the Physical Therapy room, and everyone wanted to meet them and Hero. Hero was enjoying being with Jimmy. He also liked everyone making a big deal out of him. Some of them who had gotten to know Jimmy knew about Hero and the fact he had gotten a Purple Heart.

"What a beautiful dog!"

Jimmy knew that voice; it was Fredda. "His name is Hero. He's not just a dog; he's a Veteran. He was injured in combat, and he has a Purple Heart."

"I didn't mean any disrespect. He is beautiful, though. Can I pet him?"

"I guess so."

"Jimmy, aren't you going to introduce us to this young lady?"

"Yeah, Dad. Her name is Fredda. She is one of the Physical Therapists here. Fredda, this is my mom and dad, Stan and Nancy Johnson."

"Hello. It's very nice to meet you. You must be keeping Hero for him until he gets home."

"Yes, or Hero is keeping us. He kind of runs the house. Sometimes I think he's almost human. He understands everything you say to him. He really loves Jimmy."

"I can see that, Mrs. Johnson. It's very obvious they are devoted to each other. Well, I need to get back to work. It was very nice meeting you. Jimmy, you have a great..."

"Companion," Jimmy says, cutting her off.

She smiles at his parents and leaves.

Jimmy and his parents go out to the patio to visit. "Jimmy, is there a problem with Fredda? You seem to be a little hostile toward her. She seems like a very nice girl."

"I just don't want any girls hanging around me. She was going to be my Physical Therapist, and I asked for a man instead. She's got an attitude anyway. Every time I run into her we seem to get into it. I just want her to stay away from me."

His mother speaks up. "You know it's okay to have girls who are friends, too. Is this about Sandy? Or should I ask? You're not being disloyal by being friends with a girl."

"I don't know, Mom. It just doesn't seem right. I love Sandy; no one will ever take her place. She is the love of my life." His eyes start to tear up, and he turns his head. "Let's just not talk about Fredda, okay?"

"I'm sorry son, I didn't mean to upset you."

"It's okay, Mom. Let's get out of here and I'll give you a tour of the place." Jimmy takes Hero's leash and they head out the front door.

A couple of hours later, Mr. Johnson tells Jimmy they need to head home before it gets too late. He doesn't like to drive at night. They all say goodbye and Jimmy hugs Hero and tells him he'll be home as soon as he can. As they drive off, Hero watches through the back window until he can no longer see Jimmy. He lays down in the seat and whines.

"Mrs. Johnson reaches over the seat and touches Hero. "Don't worry, Hero. The time will go by fast, and we will all have our Jimmy back home."

Chapter 52

Jimmy goes back inside after his parents and Hero have left. He feels lost and goes out to the patio. He just sits and stares at the trees, in a lonely world of his own.

Fredda sees Jimmy on the patio and goes out to try and make amends. "Hey, want some company? You look like you could use someone to talk to. I know it's hard to be away from your family. And that great, ah, Hero."

"What do you know?" Jimmy snaps at her. I've lost more than you could understand."

"Maybe," Fredda says. "But I understand loss. My husband was killed in combat. He was a Marine too. I felt lost and was so angry when he was killed I shut myself off from everyone and everything for a long time. We never had a chance to have kids, so he was my whole world."

Jimmy looks around at her and sees she has tears in her eyes. "Gee, I'm sorry. I didn't know. I lost my wife too. She was killed in an automobile accident. I'm lost without her. That's why I joined the Marines. She was, and is, the love of my life. We never had kids either. We talked about it, but we were going to wait."

"I realized – *after* I had run off almost all of my friends – that he would not want me to live like that. I went to school and studied physical therapy, then decided to come to work here. At least I can help some of these solders get their life back. Even if I can't get mine back. I guess I'd better get back inside. It's time for me to start a session." She turns to go and looks back at Jimmy. "I'm really sorry for your loss." Before Jimmy has time to say anything, she's gone.

Chapter 53

Gee. I feel like a jerk. I've been so mean to Fredda. She's lost someone she loved just like I did. I guess I'm not alone like I thought I was. It just feels like it sometimes. I need to tell her I'm sorry for the way I treated her. I never gave her a chance.

He goes back inside and looks for her, but she's busy working with a guy on the treadmill. Since he's through for the day, he heads to his room to read.

For the next two days, he doesn't see her. When he asks about her he finds out she went home for a couple of days. He figures she might be trying to avoid him since he was such a jerk.

When he is not doing physical therapy he has been doing some studying. He has taken some classes in law online and has decided he would like to be an attorney. He would like to specialize in defending the rights of children who have been mistreated or abused. He has contacted a college not far from his house and ask about their programs for GIs. He starts to take more classes with the idea that when he gets out of rehab, he will continue at the college.

"Dad, I just wanted to call and tell you what I've decided to do. I've been taking some college courses in law, and I've decided I want to be an attorney. Yeah, I know, it's a long journey to get to take the bar. But I want to do it. I'm making good progress here, and maybe in a few months I'll be home. I have found out about a program for GIs and I can qualify. What do you think?"

"That sounds great, Jimmy! I'm proud of you. You would be a good attorney; you always did like to argue. And those kids could not have a better person defending them than you. You know you can stay here as long as you want to and save money instead of paying rent. Hero already thinks he lives her. I'm sure he would share your bed with you. I wouldn't ask him to give up your old sweatshirt, though."

"Thanks, Dad. Tell Mom I love her. And tell Hero I'm thinking about him and I love him too. Talk to you later. I love you Dad."

Chapter 54

The next day Jimmy is in the library with his head stuck in a book. He feels a tap on his shoulder and looks up to see Fredda standing there. "What are you studying? You look deep in thought."

"I'm studying law. I've decided to become a lawyer. I tried to find you the other day to tell you I'm sorry for being such a jerk. I just thought I was the only one that had lost someone. I didn't want to get involved with another girl. I mean, I didn't want to be around another girl." He could feel his face turn red.

"It's okay, I understand. But I was just going to be your PT coach, that's all, not get involved with you. I, you know what I mean."

"I guess we got off on the wrong foot. Maybe we could start over." Jimmy sticks out his hand. "Hello, I'm Jimmy Johnson, it's nice to meet you."

Fredda took his hand. "Hello, I'm Fredda Moore. Glad to meet you." They both laughed. They sit and talk until it is time for lights out. "See you later, Jimmy. Have a good night."

"You too, Fredda. See you later." He felt better about himself. He had apologized. On the way back to his room he was thinking. *She's not so bad. It's nice to make a friend. Like Mom said, it's okay to have a friend who's a girl.*

Chapter 55

The next day Jimmy is working on the treadmill with his coach when Fredda walks in. "Hey, you're doing pretty good on that thing. You're going to be wanting to race me before long."

Jimmy just nods, trying not to lose concentration. When he finishes, his coach helps him back into his chair. Jimmy looks over at Fredda. "I'll even give you a head start since you're a girl." He knows he's not going to get away with that remark. He just waits for it.

Fredda laughs. "Because I'm a girl, huh? Just wait and see the back of me when I'm a long way ahead of you."

He rolls over in his chair. "They said you went home for a couple of days."

"Yeah, I went to see my mother-in-law. She's not doing too good. She has been sick with the flu for over a week. I finally convinced her to go to the hospital. She is really stubborn about going to the doctor. She thinks she can just wait it out. But she finally gave in. How is the studying going? Ready to pass the bar yet?"

"Very funny. No, but I'm hoping to go to college when I leave here. I will have to apply and take some tests to be accepted. I've been doing a lot of research online and taking some courses to get back in the swing of studying again. They have a great program for GIs near my parents home."

"That's great. You would make a great lawyer. You can be very forceful sometimes. And a good lawyer needs to be. Not that I mean you're a jerk or anything."

"Okay, I said I was sorry."

She walks off laughing.

Chapter 56

In a few minutes, Fredda returns.

"How about going out to dinner with me. We can borrow the wheelchair van. Since I am a licensed therapist, I can use it. What do you say? Just going out to dinner with a friend."

"I don't know. Is it against the rules? I mean do they care if I leave?"

"Nah, just as long as you're with me. You can tell them you need to get out of here for awhile. Believe me, they will understand. How about it?"

"I would like to have some different food for a change. Not that the food here is bad, it's just it seems to all taste alike. No matter what it is. How do you feel about Mexican food?"

"One of my favorites. There is a restaurant in town that I go to sometimes. The food is great, and it's not expensive. But it's my treat since it was my idea."

"I don't like having a girl pay for dinner. I was not raised that way. Either I pay, or I'm not going. What do you say?"

"You will definitely make a good lawyer. Okay. If you have to be a He Man, you can pay. Go tell them you're going with me and I'll go get the van and meet you out front."

“Okay, are you sure you can handle me in this chair?”

“Piece of cake. You worry too much. Just go tell them. You’re wasting time, and I’m hungry.”

Chapter 57

The ride to the restaurant doesn't take long. She parks and lowers the ramp for his wheelchair. They are given a booth. He slides out of his wheelchair and into the booth. The waiter takes his chair and puts it out of the way.

"This is nice. I haven't been out of the rehab hospital since I got there. You had a good idea. Thanks."

"I just didn't want to eat by myself." She smiles. "It's even better since you're paying."

"I knew you had a motive for asking me. Now I see." They both laugh. He stops laughing and has a funny look on his face.

"What's wrong? Did I say something wrong?"

"No, I just realized I haven't laughed in a long time. It felt good. Thanks again."

"I haven't laughed in a long time either. It is good to feel something besides sorrow and loneliness."

The waiter gets their drink order and leaves the menu. When he comes back, they are ready to order.

They talk while they eat. Not about anything special, just talk. Both feeling a sense of relief to find someone who has been through what they have. Enjoying someone's company for the first time in a long time.

He catches himself watching everything she does. He tries not to, but she is so nice and funny. He feels something funny that he doesn't understand.

Chapter 58

After they finish, and the waiter has brought the check, she reaches for the bill. He reaches for it at the same time, and his hand lands on top of hers. He looks up at her and starts to say something. She pulls her hand away and says. "I think I should at least pay my part. I ate a lot."

"Not going to happen," he says.

They both felt the spark when their hands touched. Neither wanted to acknowledge it. They just ignored it. But it was there.

When they got back to the VA, she helped him with his wheelchair then put the van back in the garage. He waited for her by the front door.

"Thanks for getting me out of here for awhile. I forgot how nice it is to have dinner with a friend."

"I enjoyed it too. I usually eat alone. It was nice to have some company. Even though Mr. He Man wouldn't let me at least pay for my dinner. It is nice to know there are still some gentlemen around. Got to go, duty calls. See you around." She smiles and walks away.

He watches her as she leaves, and notices how good her jeans fit. *She is really nice, and it is good to have a friend. Even if it is a girl.* He catches himself thinking about her.

Chapter 59

The next morning, Jimmy is back on the treadmill, working his legs without the braces. He stumbles a few times but catches himself with the bars on each side. His coach tells him to slow down and not to push so much. He gets back in stride and finishes his time. Next he works on his leg muscles with some weights on his feet. First one leg, then the other, ten on one and ten on the other. Ten on one then ten on the other.

"Do you think you're ready to try some crutches?" his coach asks.

"You think I'm ready? I'd love to get out of that wheelchair. Let me give it a try."

"Okay, now you need to learn how to use your upper body strength to pull yourself up. When you walk, your bad leg goes first, with your crutches holding your weight, then you bring your good leg forward." He takes the crutches and shows Jimmy how to pull himself up and how to use them in walking. "Got it?"

"Yeah, I think." He takes them and from sitting down tries to pull himself up. He falls back down in the chair and tries again. This time he manages to stand. "How's that, coach?"

"You did good. Just don't go too fast, or you'll end up on your face. You don't want to hurt that leg either. It's still healing, and it's going to be sore when you walk. Use the crutches to carry your weight."

Jimmy tries to take a couple of steps and almost falls. His coach catches him and gets him steady on his feet again. "Don't take such big steps. You normally wouldn't take that big of a step just walking."

Chapter 60

"Okay, trying again." He goes slower and takes small steps. This time he gets about eight steps in and stops. "This is harder than it looks. It wears out your arms and hurts your back. It's going to take some getting used to, that's for sure."

"Walk back to your chair, and we'll practice some more tomorrow. I don't want you to rush this. I know you're anxious, but you need to go slow. You're going to use muscles you haven't used before."

Jimmy gets back to his chair and thanks his coach and heads for the library. He needs some books for his on line class. He is also hoping to run into Fredda. He finds the books he is looking for, checks them out, and goes back to his room to study.

Fredda sees him heading to his room, and waits around the corner until he has gone. She is not sure how she feels about him. She has closed herself off from any feelings about another man since her husband got killed. She doesn't want to admit she felt something when their hands touched at the restaurant. He is nice, but just a friend, that's all. I have my job here and that's all I need. She is trying very hard to convince herself her one love, her husband, is the only love she will ever have.

Chapter 61

Jimmy is online taking some of the tests for his law course when he finds himself thinking about the dinner with Fredda. He shakes his head. *Concentrate! Quit thinking about her. She's a friend. You've got a lot of hard work ahead of you.* He finishes the test and closes the class for the night. When he goes to sleep, he dreams about Sandy and the time they made love in the back of his old Ford.

He wakes up with Sandy on his mind. He pulls his billfold out and looks at their wedding picture. *Why did this have to happen, Sandy? We were so happy. I feel lost without you.* He puts it away and heads to breakfast. He's thinking before long he will be out of this wheelchair. Crutches for a while, then no crutches. College, then a law degree. He had it all planned out.

As he entered the cafeteria he saw Fredda sitting with a couple of the other therapists. She looked up and saw him, and looked away. He didn't know what to think. *I wonder if I made her mad or something. I know she saw me.* He got his breakfast and sat down at one of the tables.

When she got up to leave, she walked out of her way so she wouldn't have to walk by him. *I'm not going to go out of my way to speak to her anymore. If that's the way she wants it, it's okay with me.* He finished breakfast and headed for the physical therapy room. He needed to get the hang of the crutches down. He wanted out of that wheelchair. Even more now, than before.

Chapter 62

When he got to the physical therapy room he went straight to the treadmill. He pulled himself up and went to work. His therapist saw him from across the room and walked over to him.

"What's got you fired up? You look like somebody burst your balloon."

"I'm just ready to get out of here. These walls are closing in on me. The sooner I get out of here, the sooner I can go to college and finish my law degree."

He saw Fredda come through the door out of the corner of his eye. He was determined not to look at her. He looked down at his feet and picked up his speed.

The therapist noticed how his attitude changed when Fredda walked in. He saw Jimmy glance in her direction, then look down. "You having trouble with Fredda? I thought you two got along. I saw you leave together in the van."

"Nah, she's just a little stuck up, that's all. No big deal. I don't need any woman friends anyway. I just need to concentrate on getting out of here. Okay?"

"Sure, okay with me, but you need to slow down. You're putting too much pressure on your leg. I told you to keep a good pace, not to start off at a dead run. Okay?"

"Okay. I'm ready for the crutches now." He waits while the coach gets the crutches and puts them under his arms. "Bad leg with crutches, right?"

"Yes, then swing the other one and pull the crutches forward. SLOW, okay? Just remember, if you fall, you could do some damage. That would be a setback."

Chapter 63

Jimmy starts slowly, getting the hang of it. He can feel Fredda watching him, but ignores her. He walks to the opposite end, away from her. When he gets to the wall he turns, never looking up, and walks back to his coach.

"Good job. I think a couple of more days' practice, and you'll be ready to go with the crutches full time. You feel ready?"

"Yeah, Just a little more practice. The doc says my leg is looking good. I'll still have to be careful, but if I get the hang of these things, I can think about going home. Boy am I ready." He glances in the direction of Fredda. She has her back to him working with another soldier. He hands the crutches to his coach and sits back down in his wheelchair. It's time for dinner, so he heads down to eat.

As usual, after dinner he goes to the library to do some studying. He has his head buried in a law book when he feels someone staring at him. He looks up and Fredda is sitting across the room, looking straight at him. He looks back at her, then acts like he doesn't see her. *I wonder how she likes being ignored? Two can play that game.* He picks up his books and leaves the room, not looking back.

Chapter 64

After three months, the doctor has decided Jimmy is ready to go home. He has gotten good on the crutches, and his leg is getting stronger. "Jimmy, I'm going to release you to go home at the end of the week. I want to see you one more time before you leave to check your leg and make sure the stitches are healing nicely. I'm getting your papers ready. Are you ready?"

"Yes, sir. I'm ready to go home. I've got a head start on my law degree and now I can finish at the college. They have a great Veteran's program. It's not far from my home, and my parents will take me until I'm able to drive. I can't wait to see my partner Hero. You remember him? They brought him each time they came to visit."

"Yes. He's a great dog. You're lucky to have each other. I know going into combat together gives you a bond that is like no other. I'm sure he'll be glad you're home."

The rest of the week, as far as Jimmy was concerned, went too slow. He had avoided Fredda and was hoping to leave and not see her. He was at the front door saying goodbye to some of the guys. His parents and Hero were waiting in the car for him. He was making his way down the steps and she came around the corner of the building.

"Jimmy! Wait up."

I wonder what she wants. He starts to ignore her, but his dad pointed to her to let him know who was yelling at him.

"I just wanted to say good luck in your law career. I know you've been studying hard. And I know you'll do good. When you get to be a big-time lawyer, you can come back to see all of us poor working people."

"Thanks, I've got a long way to go. But I doubt if I'll be back. I've had enough of this place. Don't work too hard." He got in the car and waved to everyone as they drove off.

Hero was all over him. He got in Jimmy's lap as much as he could, considering how big he was, and just about covered his face with big sloppy licks.

Jimmy was just as excited as Hero. He did look back, though, to see if Fredda was still standing there. She was.

Chapter 65

When they got home and put all of Jimmy's stuff was unloaded and put in his room, he finally settled down. He and Hero sat on the couch. Hero was not going to let Jimmy out of his sight.

Jimmy's mom was making dinner, and his dad sat down beside him. "We're so glad to have you home. All of us." He motioned to Hero. "You're going to take it easy for a couple of weeks before you start college, aren't you?"

"Yes, the next semester doesn't start for two weeks. I've already gotten my classes. I did that on line at the VA. I've got to get some books first thing." He props his leg up on the ottoman. "It really is good to be home. It will be good to sleep in my own bed. It wasn't bad, but there wasn't much privacy sharing a room with three other guys."

"I hope Hero lets you in your bed. He has taken it over. He might make you sleep on the floor."

"We slept in a sleeping bag together, so a bed will be a lot bigger, right Hero?" Hero is lying beside him with his head in his lap. When Jimmy mentions his name, his tail wags.

"Dinner is ready," his mom calls from the kitchen.

“Boy, I’m ready for some of mom’s cooking. The food there was okay, but nothing like hers. Come on Hero, let’s eat.” Hero hops down and is right beside Jimmy on the way to the dining room. He smells the food too. “Knowing Mom, she has made a feast. I hope she made a cherry pie.”

His dad looks at him and laughs. “Of course, she did.”

Chapter 66

A couple of days go by with Jimmy and Hero just hanging out together. Jimmy can't wait until he can drive his old Ford. His dad has been keeping it washed and tuned up for him. Every time he looks at it, he remembers the first time he and Sandy make love in the back seat. At first, it made him sad, but now it makes him smile. Along with all of the other memories he has of them together.

He spends a lot of time telling Hero about Sandy. "You would have loved her, Hero. She was the prettiest girl you'd ever see. And she had a big heart. She was good to everyone and so full of love. I really miss her. I like to think she is up there watching over us. She will watch over you too because she knows how much I love you." He shows Hero a picture of her. "See how pretty she was. When I first saw her in the hall at school, I fell in love with her. It took me a while to win her over. That was the best thing that ever happened to me, except for when I met you. That was a great day too."

Chapter 67

Later that week, Jimmy and Hero were sitting on the front porch when his phone rang. “Hello. Oh, hey, Sally. Yeah, I just got home a few days ago. How are things with you? You and Ronny still going together?”

“Yeah, we’ve been together ever since, I ah, for a long time.”

“It’s okay, Sally, you can talk about Sandy. I just try to remember all the love we had, and some of the crazy things we did together.”

“Well, we are still together. Ronny will be getting his degree soon and we’re going to get married. We both want you to come to the wedding. It’s not going to be a big one, just a few friends and our family. We are going to be in town next week and I was wondering if you would like to have lunch with us, so we could catch up.”

“Okay, that sounds great. I would like to get to know Ronny better. Especially since he’s going to marry one of my best friends. How about that Deli on 4th Street. They have a nice patio we can eat on. I have something I want to show you when we meet.”

“What is it? I love surprises. I bet your Mom and Dad were glad your home. What are you going to do now that you’re out of the Marines?”

"I've been studying law. I'm going to the University here to finish up my law degree. I want to be an attorney. I've got a lot of work to do still, but I'm determined."

"I know Sandy would be very proud of you. Hey, I've got to go, so I'll call you next week, and we can set up a time. Take care."

"Okay, looking forward to seeing you both."

Chapter 68

"Hero, that was Sandy's best friend, Sally. She and Sandy grew up together and were as close as sisters. She will be surprised to see you. You'll like her too. She is going to marry Ronny. He seems like a good guy, but I haven't been around him that much." He pulls Hero close and kisses the top of his head. "Let's go inside and find something to eat. I think mom left some of those cookies out for us."

By the end of the week, Jimmy has quit using the crutches. He asks his dad if he will go to the store with him. He wants to drive his old Ford but wants to make sure his leg won't give out on him.

"Are you sure you're ready?" his dad asks.

"I think so. If I can't make it all the way, you can take over. I'm anxious to start driving again. I hate to ask you and mom to take me places all the time. I just need to feel like I can take care of myself. I'll be starting college soon, and I'll need things every now and then. Besides I want to take Hero to the park, he needs to be able to get some exercise. It will help my leg to use it more too. I don't know how to explain it. I just need to get back to life, I guess, is what I'm trying to say. I know it will never be the same without Sandy, but Hero and I are a family now. I have been thinking about getting another apartment."

“You know you can stay here forever if you want to. We love Hero too. He has become a big part of our family, but I can understand you wanting a place of your own. Have you looked around? We can help with the finances if you find something or if you want to buy a house. That would be a good investment. You could have a back yard for Hero to run around in.”

“That’s a good idea. I really hadn’t thought about a house. I can use my VA status to get a good deal. I think I will look around. Thanks, Dad. You don’t know how much I love you and Mom. You have always been there for me. I’m lucky to have both of you. No, we’re lucky to have you. Me and Hero.”

“Your Mom and I love you and Hero. We almost went crazy when we found out you had been injured. I’m just so thankful you came home to us. Both of you.”

Chapter 69

Jimmy and Hero waited outside the deli for Sally and Ronny. When they got there he asked if Hero was welcome to sit on the patio. The owner had heard about Hero and said not only was he welcome, but that his and Jimmy's lunch was on the house. Jimmy thanked him and said he didn't want to take advantage of anyone, but the owner wouldn't take no for an answer.

Sally and Ronny both fell in love with Hero. Jimmy told them how he was the main reason his unit had gotten out alive when they were attacked from two sides. He said Hero had help drag one of the men to safety. Hero had his collar on that had the Purple Heart on it.

"How are you doing? Has your leg healed okay? Your Mom told me what happened. We've been keeping up with you through you parents."

"I'm doing great. I have finally started driving. I've still got my old ford. Dad has been keeping it in good shape for me. Hero likes to ride in the front seat with his head out the window. We go to the park, and I walk while Hero runs. He doesn't get very far away from me, though. I'm going to start to college next week. Like I told you, I'm studying for a law degree. One of the things Sandy was interested in was the kids that don't have anyone to represent them when they have been abused or just need someone to fight for them."

"That's great, Jimmy," Ronny said. "I know sometimes children's voices aren't heard because of all the red tape. I think it's a worthwhile cause to fight for."

Chapter 70

They talked for about an hour about everything.

"Are you still living at home?" Sally asked.

"Yeah, I'm thinking about buying a house. Dad said a house would be a great investment. I was going to get an apartment, but a house would give Hero a back yard of his own. I'm going to get settled in school first. Maybe mid-term I'll start to look for a house. Right now I just want to settle down and concentrate on school."

The waiter brings them their food, and after he serves them, he comes back with a tray and a plate for Hero. He sets it down in front of Hero and asks if he can pet him.

"Sure, he loves to be loved on. He's just very protective of me. Tell the owner thanks for the special treatment for Hero."

Hero looks up at Jimmy, and Jimmy says, "Go ahead, boy. Dig in." Hero doesn't need to be told twice. He cleans the plate and lays down at Jimmy's feet.

They sit and talk for a couple more hours, and Ronny says they better get going. Sally has some shopping to do. "That takes some time. She is very picky."

"Ha, ha. Very funny. I'm just particular. I know what I'm looking for, so I don't buy anything until I find it. So there."

"Okay, okay, I give up. Anyway, we better get going." He stands up and offers Jimmy his hand to shake. Jimmy reaches out and takes his hand.

"I'm glad you're taking good care of Sally. She deserves someone special." He hugs Sally, and Hero stands up. "Hero shake hands with Ronny." Hero raises his hand and shakes. "Now give Sally a kiss." Sally leans down and Hero licks her cheek.

"He's really special, Jimmy. You're very lucky to have him. And he's lucky to have you to love him so much. Take care of each other. We'll stay in touch. Don't forget we want you at our wedding. No, we want both of you at our wedding." She bends down and kisses Hero on the top of his head. "See you both later."

Chapter 71

Two weeks pass, and Jimmy is studying hard and taking as many classes as he can. He is in the library when he hears someone say his name. He looks up and doesn't recognize the face.

"Hi, I'm Dotty. You don't know me, but I saw your picture in the paper when you first came home. I wanted to say thank you for your service, and your dog Hero was very brave also. Do you still have him?"

"Hello, Dotty. Yes, I have Hero. He lives with me. I had forgotten about the picture. I didn't know they were going to do that."

"You are a local hero, and so is your dog, Hero. We are all very proud of you. I won't bother you. I just wanted to meet you. I hope someday to meet Hero. Maybe we'll run into each other someday."

"Wait, you're not bothering me. I haven't met many people here. I guess I have been too busy studying. Sit down. I have a picture of Hero if you'd like to see it."

"That would be great. The picture in the paper wasn't very good. I'll bet Hero is really smart. It said you both got a Purple Heart."

He showed Dotty the picture. "What classes do you take?" he asked her.

“I’m majoring in business. I’m in my second year. I work part-time, so it’s taking a little longer for me to finish. I work at an insurance company to learn and to make money to pay for my college.”

“What kind of Insurance company do you work for? I need to get some insurance for my old Ford. My dad has me on his policy, but I need to start getting things on my own.”

“We handle auto and home insurance. I could give you the number if you like. You can call and find out about a policy.”

“That sounds good. It’s not much, but it’s mine. What days do you work? Maybe I could come when you’re there and you could meet Hero.”

“Would you do that? I would really like to see him. I work Tuesday through Friday. I go to work at three and work until they close at five thirty.” She reaches into her purse and gets out a card. “Here is a card for the company, with the number on it. Thanks. I can’t wait to meet Hero.”

“Yeah, thanks for the information. I’ll call and set up an appointment to come in next Wednesday.

“Well, I better go and let you get back to your studying. I need to get to class too. See you.” She leaves, and he puts the card in his billfold.

Chapter 72

When Jimmy gets home, Hero is waiting at the door. Jimmy puts his books down and kneels and hugs Hero. His mother comes in and tells Jimmy Hero sits by the door when he knows it's time for him to come home. "I think he has a clock in his head, and it goes off about ten minutes before you get home. That's when he heads for the door."

Jimmy tells his mother about meeting Dotty. "I need to start getting things in my name so I can start building my own credit history. That way when I get ready to buy a house, I will have some credit already. That will help me get started."

"You don't have to hurry, Jimmy. We don't mind having you on our policy."

"I know, Mom, but I need to start standing on my own two feet. We'll be in my room if you need help with dinner. Is Dad still at the store?"

"Yes, he told Paul he would close tonight. Paul's wife is expecting, and he gave him the night off. He'll be home around six-thirty. Are you hungry? I can fix you a snack."

"No, thanks. I'll just wait for dinner. Come on, Hero, we need to study."

Chapter 73

After classes, Jimmy heads downtown to the insurance company. He stops by his house to pick up Hero. His appointment is at four o'clock. He parks his old Ford two spaces down from the front door. When he walks in, Dotty greets him.

"Hello, Jimmy. Oh my gosh, this must be Hero." She gets up from her desk and walks around to where Jimmy and Hero are standing. "Is it okay if I pet him?"

"Sure. Hero, shake hands with Dotty. She goes to the same college I go to." Hero raises his paw and shakes Dotty's hand.

"He is beautiful, Jimmy. I told my boss about you and Hero, and he's anxious to meet you both. Have a seat and I'll tell him you're here." She goes to the back and comes out with her boss.

Mr. Bailey, meet Jimmy Johnson. He would like to get some insurance for his truck."

Mr. Bailey shakes Jimmy's hand. "Dotty told me about you two. I'm honored to meet both of you." He kneels down and Hero holds up his paw to shake. "It's nice to meet you, Hero. If you two will follow me into my office, we can talk about insurance for you."

Chapter 74

When all of the papers are signed, and they get back to Dotty's desk, she is still there. Jimmy tells her he appreciates her help. He asks if she has plans for dinner. He says he and Hero are going to grab a burger and asks if she would like to go with them. He figures since she went to all this trouble for him he could repay her with a burger.

"I'd love to Jimmy. I usually eat alone or just take something back to my apartment. Let me get my computer shut down and I'll be out in a minute." She finishes getting everything done for the night and meets Jimmy and Hero outside. He is waiting by his Ford. "This is a neat truck. I love old cars and trucks. Have you had it long?"

"Yeah, a long time." He immediately thinks of Sandy. He opens the door for her, and Hero jumps into the back seat. "Is Minute Burger okay with you? I really like their burgers and they have a patio where Hero and I like to sit."

"That sounds great. I've eaten there, and I like their burgers too. Thanks for the invite. I didn't know what I was going to do for dinner."

Chapter 75

They arrive at the Minute Burger, and Jimmy opens the door for her and Hero. He asks her what kind of burger she wants, and he orders for all three of them. They sit on the patio. When their order is ready a girl brings a tray out with their food. Jimmy gives Dotty hers first, then puts Hero's down for him. "He only gets meat and bread. The rest isn't really good for him. I watch what he eats."

"I can tell you love him. And it's mutual, I can also tell. You're lucky to have each other. I love dogs, but I can't have a dog at my apartment. Someday, I'll have a house, and I'm going to get one. That's the plan anyway. Didn't you tell me you live with your mom and dad?"

"Yeah. Until I get finished with college and pass the bar. It helps with the expenses. I'm thinking about getting a house when I finish, as an investment. That way Hero can have his own backyard. He loves Mom and Dad's. He likes to chase the birds. He can't catch them; it's just the chase. It gives him good exercise."

They sit and talk for a couple of hours then he takes her back to her office to get her car.

Chapter 76

On his way home, he thinks. *Dottie's really nice. It was fun to have someone to talk to. It wasn't really a date. Maybe she would like to go to a movie sometime. I don't ever go anywhere, and she's easy to talk to. I guess I could ask her. Just as friends. If I see her on the campus, I'll ask her. I don't need to get involved with anyone. We could just be friends. I've got too much ahead of me to get involved. A lot of heavy studying.*

His mom is in the den, watching TV when he gets home. "Did you get your insurance all taken care of? You know it was okay for you to stay on our policy. I don't want you to have too much to worry about. You still have a lot of work to do to pass the bar."

"It's okay, Mom. It's no big deal. I need to start doing things for myself. The girl I met at school works there. She went to get a burger with Hero and me. She's nice and easy to talk to. I was thinking I might ask her to go to a movie sometime if I run into her on campus."

"That's a good idea. You need to do something besides studying all the time. It would be good for you to go out some. You need to meet some people your own age to hang out with."

"Well, I don't get to meet too many people. I think like me everyone is busy studying and I spend a lot of time in the library doing research. Speaking of studying, I need to do some. I'll be in my room if you need any help with dinner."

"Okay, Sweetheart. Your dad will be home around five-thirty, so we'll eat around six."

Chapter 77

A couple of weeks go by, and Jimmy has not seen Dotty. He decides to go by the insurance company. He and Hero are walking in when Dotty is leaving.

"Hi. Are you off work?"

"Yeah, I've been working extra hours. We've been busy, so Mr. Bailey told me to take off early. Do you need anything?" She bends down to pet Hero.

"I was just thinking I might go to a movie tomorrow night. I was wondering if you might want to go? It's a new space movie. Do you like space movies?"

"I like most movies. Just not scary ones. That would be great. I'd love to go."

"I would like it if we could be friends. It was nice talking to you the other day. You're like me. You don't have much free time with working and going to college."

"I would like that. It is nice to have a friend to talk to. And you're right, I don't have a lot of free time."

"If you give me your address, I can pick you up. I'll see what time the movie starts and call you. Oh, I don't have your phone number." He gets his phone out and asks her to give him her number so he can put it in his phone.

"Okay, I'll call you tomorrow, and we can set a time. Okay?"

"Okay. What about Hero? Will they let him in the movie?"

"Na. He'll have to stay with my mom and dad. They love to have him there. They pretty much spoil him anyway. And he loves it. Okay, see you tomorrow night."

"Bye, Hero."

Chapter 78

Jimmy gets in his truck and decides to go for a drive just to get out for a while. He finds himself at the lake where he and Sandy used to go. He parks, He and Hero get out and walk down to the water's edge.

Hero feels like something is wrong, Jimmy seems sad. Hero picks up a stick and nudges Jimmy's leg.

"Not now, Hero. I need to think some." Jimmy goes over to the bench and sits down.

Hero drops the stick and follows him over to the bench. He puts his head on Jimmy's knee and looks up at him.

"I'm not sure I should have asked Dotty to go to the movie. I told her we were just friends. That's all I want is to be friends. I don't want to replace Sandy. I can't replace Sandy. She was the one for me. You would have loved her, Hero. She would have loved you too, just like I do." He bends over and holds Hero in his arms. He feels tears on his cheeks. Hero feels Jimmy's pain and snuggles closer. They sit together until almost dark, then head home.

Chapter 79

When they walk in the door, his mom and dad are about to eat dinner. "I was wondering if you were going to make it home for dinner." She looks at Jimmy and sees in his eyes how sad he is. "Is something wrong?" She asks.

Jimmy's dad stops before he sits down. "What's wrong, Son?"

Jimmy puts his arms around his mother. "It's just I miss Sandy so much. I went to our spot at the lake today. That's where we've been. I just can't seem to let go. Even though it's been three years, it seems like it just happened yesterday. I asked Dotty to go to the movie with me tomorrow night, and I feel guilty. I was thinking of calling her and telling her I can't go."

His mother says, "Let's sit down a minute; the dinner will keep." She goes over to the couch and Jimmy and his Dad follow. "I know you miss Sandy; we do too. We loved her too, but she wouldn't want you to stop living. What you had was something special, a love that not everyone experiences. You can't close yourself off from life. You're not being disloyal to her by having a relationship with someone else."

"You will always have her in your heart," his dad says. "But there is room enough in there for someone else someday. It may take a long time to get there, but she would want you to."

"I know you're both right, it's just hard to look at anyone else and not see Sandy. Dotty is really nice. I told her I would like for us to be friends, and she is okay with that. I guess I'm the one who has the problem. I thought it would get easier, but it doesn't seem to. I still feel this hole in my heart."

"You don't have to jump into anything, just be friends. If the right one comes along, you'll know it. Sandy would want you to be happy." His dad pats him on the shoulder.

"Okay. Just one day at a time. Isn't that how the saying goes? I'll try it. I guess I'll go tomorrow night. Just friends." He gets up and hugs his mother and daddy. "I guess I've ruined dinner."

"No, you haven't. I was just about to put it on the table. You and Hero wash up and come down to eat. Okay?"

"Yes, Ma'am."

Chapter 80

Jimmy picks up Dotty, and they head to the movie.

When they get to the ticket counter, Dotty says, “I think I should pay for my ticket. We’re going as friends, and you should not pay for me too.”

“I asked you to go with me. Even though we are friends, it was my invite, so I’m paying. Okay?”

“Only if you let me buy the popcorn and drinks. Okay?”

“You drive a hard bargain, Dotty, but okay.”

On the way home from the movie, Jimmy asks Dotty how things are going in her classes. “I’m doing pretty good, but there is a lot to understand and remember.”

“How is your law study going? How much longer do you have before you can pass the bar?”

“I have a couple of more years. I did some online courses while I was at rehab. Now I am taking extra classes to catch up.”

“Why did you decide to be an attorney? And what kind of an attorney are you going to be?”

Jimmy sits there for a while before answering.

“I’m sorry, it’s none of my business. I was just curious.”

“No, it’s okay. I was married for a while. My wife always wanted to help abused or neglected children who didn’t have a voice. I thought I would do it for her. She was killed in an accident about three years ago.”

“I’m so sorry, Jimmy. I wasn’t trying to pry. I’m really sorry.”

“I’m trying to learn to live without her. That’s why I joined the service. I was running away, I guess. But now I have Hero, and he helps me get from one day to the next.”

He pulls up in front of her apartment. “I hope I didn’t ruin things. I didn’t mean to bring all of that up. “

“No, you didn’t. I should not have asked so many questions. I did enjoy the evening. Thank you for inviting me. I guess I’ll see you at school. Tell Hero I said hello.” She starts to get out of the car.

“Hey, thanks for listening and being a friend. See you, and I’ll tell Hero you said hello.”

Chapter 81

Jimmy sees Dotty on campus now and then but is concentrating on his studies. He starts looking for a part-time job and goes to the garage he used to work for to see if Mel has an opening.

"Hey, Jimmy! I was wondering if you were going to stop by and see me. I heard you were wounded. Are you okay now? And who is this beautiful dog?'

"Hi, Mel. This is Hero. He was my partner in combat. Hero, say hello to Mel."

Hero raises his paw to shake with Mel.

"I'm okay now. I had to go through rehab. I'm going to college to become a lawyer. I was looking for a part-time job. I don't suppose you need anyone, do you?"

"Hey, you were the best mechanic I had. I could use you. I do a lot of the work myself even with Doug, who's pretty good, I can't keep up. When could you start? How about Monday? That will give me time to get the paperwork done. It will be good to have you back."

"Monday is fine. I will just have to have time for my classes, but I can work around them if that's okay."

"Sure, and you can bring Hero with you if you want to. He can stay in the office. I'll fix him a bed."

"He'd like that. He goes almost everywhere with me. Okay, I'll see you Monday."

Chapter 82

He goes home and tells his mom and dad about the job.

"Are you sure you're not taking on too much, with your school and all?"

"No, it's okay, Dad. Mel said he would let me work around my school schedule. I can use the extra money too. I want to start saving up for a house. When the time comes, with my GI Bill, I can get a good deal. But I want to have money to fix it up too. My old truck won't last forever. One day I'll have to think about getting either another truck or a car. It will be hard to give up my truck, it has a lot of memories. I think I'm going to go take a quick shower before dinner. I'll be down in a few minutes."

"I hope Jimmy is not pushing himself too much, getting a job," said Jimmy's mother.

"He's a big boy, Honey. You need to let him decide things for himself."

"I know, but he's still my little boy. You know how mothers are. It's my job to worry about him."

Chapter 83

A year goes by, and Jimmy is getting closer to his dream of becoming a lawyer. He is still working for Mel at the garage.

"Hey Jimmy, Jackie and I are going to have some friends over for a barbecue this Saturday night. I would really like for you to come. What do you say? Nothing fancy, just a few friends. You can bring someone if you like. I don't know if you're dating or not. If you are, you can bring her."

"Nah, I'm not dating anyone. I've been too busy, as you well know. When I'm not in class, I'm here working, or home studying. What time, and can I bring anything?"

"Nope, just bring yourself. Around six thirty. You remember where I live?"

"Yeah. I remember. Thanks."

"Okay, see you Saturday night."

Friday night, Jimmy's dad asks him if he wants to go out to dinner with them Saturday night. They are going to try the new Mexican food place downtown.

"Thanks, Dad. I'm going over to Mel's house; they're having a barbecue. I won't be out late, but I told him I'd come. Some of the guys from the garage are going too."

"I'm glad you're getting out. All you do is study. But it won't be long before I have a lawyer for a son just in case I get into any trouble."

"Like I can see you getting into trouble. That would be the day."

"Have you seen Dotty any since the movie?"

"No. I just don't feel like dealing with anything, not even as a friend."

"Just don't shut yourself off. There might be someone out there for you. You need to have some fun and enjoy life again. You're still young and good-looking, like your dad."

"I second that," Jimmy's mom chimed in. "You *are* good-looking like your dad. I thought he was gorgeous forty years ago, and I still think so today. He's still my love."

"You two are too much. I love you both. But let's not get mushy on me."

Chapter 84

"Hey, Mel."

"Hi, Jimmy. Glad you could make it. Hi, Hero. Glad you're here too. Everyone is out in the back yard; go on out. I'm just going to get some more hamburgers, and I'll be out. Jackie is out there; she can introduce you to anyone you don't know."

Jimmy walks out in the yard and hugs Jackie, Mel's wife.

"Hi, Jimmy. Good to see you. This must be Hero." She leans down and pets Hero. "He's beautiful. Hello, Hero."

"Jimmy, we're so glad you're back home and safe. I was sorry to hear about your being wounded. I heard Hero was wounded also."

"Yeah, we both spent some time in the hospital, but we're okay now. Thanks for the invite. I see some people I know and …."

"What is it, Jimmy?" She turns to see who he is looking at. "That's Fredda. She's my niece. She's pretty, isn't she? She used to work at the rehab hospital where you were sent. I'm surprised you didn't meet her there. Her red hair is something, isn't it? Would you like me to introduce you to her?"

"There's no need. I met her when I was at the rehab hospital. She was one of the physical therapists. She's your niece?"

"Yes, she left the hospital about six months ago. She said she just wanted a change. I'm not sure what made her change her mind; she was always so happy there. She lost her husband in combat. She is kind of a loner. You said you met her? You should go say hello. She just moved here and doesn't know many people. As I said, she pretty much keeps to herself. Get something to drink. Mel is motioning for me; he must need some help. Enjoy yourself."

Chapter 85

Jimmy is staring at Fredda when she turns around and sees him. She quickly turns back the other direction away from him. He walks over to her and taps her on the shoulder. "Hey. Small world, huh?"

"Yes, too small. Hello, Hero." She bends down to love on him, then looks up at Jimmy. "What are you doing here? I guess you know Mel and Jackie."

"Yeah, I work for Mel part time. I worked for him before I went into the Marines. Jackie said you left the hospital. I thought you said that was where you wanted to be, to help the wounded."

"It was; I just needed a change. Some of the wounded don't want help. They were almost rude when you tried to get to know them. If you will excuse me, I am going to see if Uncle Mel needs some help." She visibly brushes him off and walks away.

He's thinking to himself. *Boy, she still has an attitude. Why is she so upset. I didn't do anything. I just said hello. Oh well, her problem, not mine.*

Chapter 86

"Hey Doug, what's going on. Hi Jerry, you guys been here long?"

"Not long. Cool, you brought Hero. Hey Hero, what happening, kid." He pets Hero on the head. "I saw you talking to Fredda. She's kind of stuck up. I tried to ask her out once, she said she wasn't interested in dating. She's Mel's niece. She just moved here about a month ago. You're wasting your time if you're interested."

"Not interested, just saying hello. I met her at the VA. She was one of the physical therapists. She lost her husband in combat. She's okay. Maybe she just wants to be left alone. I thought you were going with someone."

"I was, but she was getting too serious. I'm not ready to settle down yet. I'm too young and good looking to share this with just one girl."

"Hah! If you say so."

"Are you dating anyone? I know you're going to the university and working part time, I just wondered. I've got a date this weekend with a neat girl. I could see if she has a friend if you like."

"Nah, that's okay. No time for that. I still have a long way to go before I can graduate and take the bar exam. Between school and work and study, I barely have time to sleep and eat. Guess I'm just not there yet."

"I'm sorry, I should not have said anything about dating. I know what happened with Sandy. I'm really sorry, man. I didn't mean to bring up any bad memories."

"It's okay. Don't worry about it. I will start dating someday if the right one comes along. But for now, I'm just into work and school."

Chapter 87

Mel comes out with a tray of hamburger patties. “Okay everybody, burgers going on the grill. Get something to drink and a plate. The burgers will be ready soon.” He goes over to the grill and starts the patties. “Hey Jimmy, did you finish that assignment you were working on?”

“Finished it last night. It was hard. You need any help with those?”

“Got it covered. Did you meet my niece Fredda? She worked at the rehab hospital. Might have been there when you were. Here she comes, I'll introduce you. Fredda, come over here. I want you to meet someone.”

“Wait, Mel. I, ah, already know her.”

“Uncle Mel, Jimmy, and I met before. Hello Jimmy. I need to go help Aunt Jackie inside.”

“That's strange. She is usually very friendly. Did you say you met at the the rehab hospital? It's none of my business, but did something happen between you two?”

“Not really. We just didn't get along, that's all. When are those burgers going to be ready? I'm hungry.”

Chapter 88

A week passes, Jimmy and Hero are at the park. Hero chases some balls Jimmy brought with him. Jimmy throws one and it lands in the middle of a blanket where someone is reading. Hero runs after it and stops before he steps on the blanket. Jimmy is running after him to keep him from bothering the person there.

"Hero! What are you doing here? Is this yours?" The woman hands the ball to Hero and looks up to see Jimmy running toward her.

"Fredda? Sorry, I didn't mean to throw it that far. I hope it didn't hit you. I'm really sorry." Hero is standing there with the ball in his mouth. Jimmy takes the ball and throws it again. Hero runs off to get it.

"It's okay. It didn't hit me. It just scared me when it hit. You need to be more careful; you could hurt someone."

"Are you always this mad, or is it just me you're always mad at?"

"It's just you. You made it clear at the rehab hospital that you don't want to be friends and that's okay with me. Now, if you don't mind, I was reading."

"Well, I wouldn't want to interrupt your reading. Hero! Let's go, boy." He takes the ball Hero has brought back and walks to his car.

"Let's go home, Hero. This park is too crowded." He looks back at Fredda, who has gone back to her book. *I almost feel sorry for her. She seems so sad and alone. Her choice, I guess. Not my problem.*

Fredda puts her book down and watches as Jimmy drives away. *What a jerk. I thought when I first met him, he was nice. Boy, was I wrong!* She tries not to think about him, but can't seem to get back to her book. Then she starts to think about the husband she lost, and the pain. *How can I ever get past the hurt? I miss him so much.*

Chapter 89

The following week Jimmy sees Dotty at the cafeteria. He hesitates to speak, but she sees him and waves him over to her table.

"Hi Jimmy, did you just get here? Why don't you get your food and sit here with me?"

"Yeah. Just walked in. Okay, I'll be right back."

"How is Hero? He's so beautiful

"He's fine. He stays with mom and dad when I'm at school. Are you still busy at the insurance agency?

"Yes, we've been really busy. It's time for a lot of policies to renew, so there is a lot of paperwork. Between that school and studying, I barely have time to sleep."

They eat in silence for a while. Then Dotty asks, "I've been invited to a party next weekend, and I was wondering if you would like to go with me. It's not a big deal. One of my girlfriends is having a birthday party for her boyfriend. It's on Saturday night, and it starts at eight o'clock. Would you like to go?"

Jimmy sits there for a minute before he answers. "Ah, I ah, guess so. I haven't actually gone on a date with anyone. I mean as a date. Not like when we went to the movie."

"Oh, it's okay if you'd rather not. I just thought we could go as friends, like we did at the movie, but it's okay. I understand."

"No, I mean, I guess it could be a date. I'd like that. We get along, and you're easy to talk to. Okay?"

"Okay. You know where I live. Pick me up around seven-thirty? And it's not a dress-up thing. Just jeans. You might know some of the people there from school. I think it will be fun."

"I hate to run, but my class starts in a few minutes, and I need to go. I guess I'll see you Saturday night."

"Yeah, see you Saturday."

Dotty leaves and Jimmy sits there, wondering what he has done. *A date? What is wrong with me? I don't need to date. I have all my studying to do. I should not have said I would go. I'm stuck now. I can't back out; it would hurt her feelings. I guess I'm going to a party Saturday night.*

Chapter 90

After school, when Jimmy gets home, Hero is waiting at the door.

His mother asks how school went.

"I'm afraid I've gotten myself into a mess."

"What happened? What do you mean a mess?"

"You remember I told you about Dotty, the girl I met at school. She and I went to a movie together. Now she has asked me to go to a party Saturday night and I said yes. It's a date. Now I'm not sure I want to go. What should I do?"

"You should go and have fun. You need to start to have a life, Jimmy. It's time you let go of Sandy. I don't mean to forget her; I mean start to live again. Go on dates and have some fun. She would want you to. If it was you who died, wouldn't you want her to go on living and be happy?"

"Yes. I always wanted her to be happy. I guess if it were me, I would have wanted her to find someone else and be happy. Okay, I'll try. Dotty is nice. Come on Hero, we've got some studying to do."

Chapter 91

Saturday night Jimmy pulls up in front of Dotty's apartments. He sits there for a few minutes then takes a deep breath and gets out. He knocks on her front door.

"Just a minute," a voice calls from inside. The door opens,. "Come on in. I just need to get my purse. I'm glad you decided to go. I think you'll enjoy it. They are a great bunch of people."

"You look nice, Dotty. And thanks for inviting me. I guess I just don't get out much. My mom said I should. If I'm not at school, I'm at work or home studying."

"Everybody needs to have some fun. It's not good to work all of the time. Okay, I'm ready. Let's go."

They arrive, and the party is going strong. Dotty seems to know everyone there. She introduces Jimmy and he sees a few people he knows. Doug is there and comes over to say hello.

"Hey man, glad to see you here. Is Dotty your date? She's really nice. I've known her for a long time. She dated a friend of mine a while back."

"Yeah, she invited me at school last week. I finally decided to start dating. It just took me some time to decide it was time. I'm glad you're here, at least I know a few people. Is Jerry here?"

"Yeah, somewhere. He brought a date. Her name is Anna. She's cool. I came alone so I could check all the chicks out to see who would be the lucky one to get me."

"Just as modest as always, I see. Have you decided who this lucky girl will be yet?"

"Still looking. Hey, there is Miss Stuck-up herself. Maybe I'll give her another chance to be the lucky one."

Chapter 92

Jimmy looks and sees Fredda standing by the door. He sees Doug approach her, and watches to see what happens. She shakes her head no, and Doug walks away. She turns and sees Jimmy. She smiles, then she sees Dotty go over to Jimmy and hand him a soda. She quickly turns away.

"I brought you a soda. I saw you talking to Doug. How do you know him?"

"I work at the garage for Mel where he works."

"I've known him a long time. I dated a friend of his a few months ago. Doug and I met at another party a couple of years ago, and have been friends ever since. He's a good guy; just loves the girls. The girls all call him Casanova. He thinks he is anyway." They both laugh.

Jimmy glances over to see Fredda talking to Jerry. She shakes her head, and he kind of shrugs his shoulders and walks away. *Guess he struck out too.*

Later that night, he is getting another soda and Fredda walks up and says hello.

"Hi. Need a soda?"

"No, just saying hello. You with Dotty? I didn't know you knew her. She hangs out with some of the people I used to. This is the first time I've been to one of their parties. I saw you talking to Doug and Jerry. I guess you know them too."

"I work with Doug, and I've known Jerry for a couple of years."

Dotty walks up. "I didn't know you two knew each other."

They both start to speak at the same time.

Fredda says, "Go ahead," and stops talking.

"We met at the rehab hospital. She was one of the physical therapists."

"Oh, I didn't think about that. What are you doing now, Fredda?"

"I'm just taking some time off. I haven't decided what I'm going to do next. Well, I think I'll head home. I don't usually stay out this late. You two have a good time."

"See you, Fredda" Jimmy and Dotty both say.

"She is pretty much a loner since she lost her husband. I feel sorry for her. It must be hard to lose someone you...Oh, I'm sorry. I didn't think."

"It's okay. I do know how she feels. It's hard to start again. It seems the hurt never really goes away."

Midnight rolls around and they tell everybody goodbye and leave. Jimmy drives Dotty home and walks her to the door. After she opens it, she asks him if he would like to come in.

"It's late, and I think I should go home. I need to finish a paper I'm working on. I had a nice time; thanks again for inviting me." He doesn't know whether he should kiss her or not, so she stands on her tiptoes and kisses him. He just stands there for a second, then kisses her back. They look at each other for a few minutes, then they start to laugh. "I guess we should just stay friends."

"Yeah, let's just stay friends.

"Are you sure you don't want to come in for a while. I could make us some hot chocolate."

"Maybe for a while. Are you sure?"

"Yeah, we can just sit and talk. It's nice to have a friend to talk to." She opened the door and they went in. She made hot chocolate and they laughed about the kiss.

He thought he would feel guilty going out with someone else. Instead, he felt as if he was starting to finally let go of Sandy.

Chapter 93

"I like the way you make hot chocolate." They both laughed.

"I don't make hot chocolate for everyone. I think you're special. It's been a long time since I just sat down and talked with a friend. I was engaged, and he broke it off. His parents thought I wasn't good enough for him. They had money, and I was just a poor peasant. That's my sad story."

"You're a great person. Apparently, he was not too bright, or he wouldn't have let you go. You're better off if he was that much of a fool to let his parents decide who he should marry. It's been a long time for me too. I haven't really talked to anyone since Sandy died.

Jimmy looked around, "You have a nice apartment." I need to find one for me and give my parents a rest from me. They say it's not a bother, but Hero and I need our own space. If I pass the Bar, I'm thinking of buying a house. Hero could have his own back yard, and it would be a good investment."

"That sounds like a plan." She sets the hot chocolate on the table and sits down. "I think you should say, when I pass the bar, not *if* I pass the bar. I know you will. You've been studying so hard, and you're really dedicated."

"Thanks for the vote of confidence. I just need another year, and I can take the test. It will be worth all the hard work if – okay, *when* I pass the bar."

They drink their hot chocolate and talk for about an hour. Jimmy looks at his watch. "I guess I'd better go home. I bet my mom and dad are worried. Even though they say to come and go as I please, I bet they stayed up late tonight waiting for me.

"Thanks again for the hot chocolate." He smiles at her then touches her cheek. "You're a good friend Dotty. "I'll see you at school."

"I'm glad you went with me. I had a good time too." She smiles. "See you at school."

Chapter 94

Jimmy tries to sneak up the stairs when he hears a voice. "Glad you're home safe."

He sees his parents' bedroom door is cracked open. "Thanks, Mom. You shouldn't wait up for me. In case you haven't noticed, I'm not seventeen anymore."

"You're still my little boy, no matter how old you are. Good night, Son."

"Good night, Mom."

"Good night, Son."

"You too, Dad? Good night."

Hero is waiting in Jimmy's bed. He sits up, and his tail goes wild. Jimmy hugs him and sits down beside him. "Did you miss me tonight? I went to a party and then went to Dotty's apartment. We had some hot chocolate, and it was great. I haven't had hot chocolate in a long time."

Hero is licking his face. "Hey, let me get my clothes off and I'll get in bed." When he starts to get in, Hero is laying across the bed. "Hero, I hate to be picky, but you can't have the whole bed." He pushes him over to the side. "That's your side, this is mine. And no snoring." Hero gets up and lays with his head across Jimmy's stomach. "Good night boy, I love you." He lays his hand on Hero's head and goes to sleep.

Chapter 95

Jimmy wakes up thinking about his new friendship with Dotty. She is a really neat girl. We can just be friends, and that's good for both of us.

Down at breakfast, his mom is cooking and he sets the table. His dad comes in and asks him how the party went.

"It was good. I met some new people and saw some I knew. I think it was good for me to get out. I'm going to try to open up some to other things. I have been so shut off I forgot what it's like to have a good time. Dotty is nice, but we have decided we are just good friends. I don't want to get involved with anyone until I pass the bar. Notice I said *when* I pass the bar. I'm determined to be a lawyer and defend kids who need someone to stand up for them. I should be able to take the test in another year. I've doubled up on my classes and am working really hard."

"That's good, son. Just don't wear yourself out. And I'm glad you had a good time. It's good to have a friend to talk to and do things with. You're lucky you met Dotty."

"I think after breakfast, Hero and I are going to the park. He needs some exercise. I've been so busy; I haven't spent enough time with him."

Chapter 96

Jimmy and Hero climb into his old truck and head for the park. He parks in the same spot and lets Hero out. He finds a bench and watches Hero run around, never getting very far from Jimmy.

"Hello. Isn't that Hero?" A man asks as he walks up.

"Yes, how did you know?"

"We remember seeing his picture in the paper with you. My name is Dale, this is my wife, Elaine. And this is Daisy. Rescue dogs are the best dogs. They appreciate the love and attention they never received before. We got her from the shelter in town."

Elaine looks lovingly down at Daisy. "Yeah, we thought about a dog from the animal store but decided to get a rescue. I'm glad we did. She's the best."

"I guess Hero thinks so too. They are playing together. He doesn't get much time with other dogs. My name is Jimmy, by the way. Do you come here often?"

"We try to get out at least every two weeks. We both work, and sometimes the days get away from us. We do try to just relax. That's where the park comes in."

"I know the feeling. I go to college, and it seems all I do is work and study."

"What are you studying?"

I'm studying law. I want to be an attorney. I have a little over a year before I can take the bar. I try to bring Hero here at least every couple of weeks. More if I can." Jimmy finds himself looking around for Fredda. She's not in the spot where she was last week.

"Well, it's time for us to go. Hope you and Hero enjoy the day. It's a pretty one. See you around. Come on, Daisy, time to go home." Daisy and Hero both come running up to them. Dale puts a leash on Daisy and the three of them leave.

Chapter 97

Hero is sitting there waiting for Jimmy to throw the ball. "Okay, fellow, here you go."

He throws it in the same spot where Fredda was sitting last time. She is still not there. After about an hour, he gathers up Hero and leaves. They drive down through town with Hero's head sticking out the window. It's almost lunchtime so he decides to go through the Piedmont and get him and Hero a burger. He orders and the carhop brings out the sack with a burger for Jimmy and a patty for Hero.

"Let's take our lunch back to the park. It's such a pretty day, might as well sit on the bench and eat. Right?" Hero just sits and stares at the bag. Jimmy parks back in the same spot. He walks up to the bench and sits down. He tosses Hero his patty and opens up his burger. He looks around just to see who is there.

From behind him, he hears someone say, "Hello, Hero." He recognizes the voice; it's Fredda.

"Hi, Fredda. I was just about to have a burger. I'll share if you want. I'm afraid Hero doesn't share. His is already gone."

"It's okay. I've already eaten. I was just going to do some reading. I brought my blanket. I'll see you." She goes over to her spot, lays out her blanket, leans against a tree, and starts reading.

Chapter 98

Jimmy finishes his burger and walks over to her. What are you reading?"

"A mystery. But I usually figure out who did it before I finish the book. It's kind of like a challenge. Just to see if I'm right."

"Do you mind if I sit with you?"

"I guess not."

"I want to apologize for being such a jerk at the rehab hospital. I was angry and so wrapped up in getting better and getting out of there. I was also worried about Hero. At least that's my excuse. I just didn't want to talk to anyone."

"I know the feeling. After I lost Mark, I kind of shut myself off from the world. I got so tired of everyone feeling sorry for me and telling me they knew how I felt. They had no idea how I felt."

"That's the way I was. No one could know what it's like to lose someone who's such a part of you. It's like there is this big hole in your heart and you don't know what to do about it. You keep thinking it will go away, and it just doesn't."

"Yeah, and you get angry and upset and have all these feelings you don't know what to do with. So, you just shut down. I'm afraid I was a jerk too. I went to work there to help the soldiers, and yet I also needed help. I finally decided to go talk to someone. I went for counseling, but that really didn't help. I ah, can't believe I'm talking about Mark. I haven't talked to anyone about him. I don't usually talk at all."

"I don't either. Since I lost my wife Sandy, I haven't opened up to anyone. It feels like you do understand. It's strange how much our lives are similar. I fell in love with Sandy the first time I saw her. She didn't even know I existed. It took me two weeks to get up the courage just to speak to her."

"When Mark first asked me out, I was shocked. He was a big football hero, and I wasn't anything. After the first date, I decided he was the boy I wanted to marry. We got married after he finished boot camp. We had only been married a little over a year when he...when I lost him." She looked away so he wouldn't see the tears on her cheeks.

Chapter 99

Hero picked up his ball and walked over to Fredda and dropped it in her lap.

"He knows you're sad. He thinks playing ball makes him happy, so maybe it will make you happy too."

"Okay, Hero. Let's play ball." She stands up and throws the ball. He chases after it, and when he brings it back, she throws it again.

Jimmy watches her. Her red hair is pulled back into a ponytail, shining under her baseball cap. She looks around at him and laughs. For the first time, he notices she has beautiful, emerald green eyes. *Red hair and green eyes, a good combination.*

"Wow, he can wear you out. I need to sit down."

"Yeah, he has a lot of energy. Sometimes I can't keep up with him. He likes to chase the ball. At Mom and Dad's, he chases the birds. But they're too fast, even for him."

"Well, I guess I better go. I promised Aunt Jackie I would come for dinner. I need to go home and change before I go. I guess I'll see you sometime. Thanks for listening. And Hero, thanks for playing ball with me. It did cheer me up."

"See you. Tell Mel and Jackie I said hi."

He watches her as she walks off. He likes the way her jeans fit, and he thinks about her green eyes.

Chapter 100

It's a couple of weeks before Jimmy and Hero go back to the park. They play ball, and Jimmy waits for about an hour, but no Fredda. He finally gives up and leaves. Fredda had seen Jimmy sitting on the bench, but after opening up so much about Mark and her feelings, she felt uneasy. He was getting in her head, and it worried her. He was getting through the walls she had built up. It scared her. She wasn't sure she was ready to get close to anyone. Especially Jimmy. He made her feel too much., so she left without saying anything to him.

Jimmy works hard on his law classes. It's been about three months since he has run into Fredda. He has decided she just doesn't want to get close with anyone. He still goes to the park, but it's just to give Hero exercise, or that's what he tells himself.

Chapter 101

He and Dotty have gotten to be good friends.

"Hey Dotty, what are you doing? Want to take in a movie tomorrow night?"

"Sure. What's showing? I hope it's that new Sci-Fi movie, War of the Planets. You want me to meet you there?"

"No, I'll pick you up. If you want to, we can get a pizza first. I like Leo's Pizza; it's on the way to the movie."

"That sounds good, I love pizza. What time do you want me to be ready?"

"I'll be there around six. That will give us plenty of time to eat and still make the movie on time."

"I'll be ready. I want to go Dutch, though. Since we're just friends, I don't want you to pay my way. Okay?"

"You are really hard-headed. Okay, if it's that big of a deal. See you tomorrow night."

They walk into Leo's Pizza and find a table. Just as they order, Fredda walks in. "Hey Fredda, Come and sit with us." Dotty waves from their table. "We just ordered."

Jimmy stands up and pulls the chair out for Fredda. The waitress takes her order. "I was going to get my pizza to go," Fredda says as she looks at Jimmy.

"We're going to the movies, why don't you go with us? It's that new Sci-Fi movie, War of the Planets," Jimmy tells Fredda. "It's going to be a good movie."

"I don't want to interrupt your date. I'll just take my pizza home."

Dotty laughs. "It's not a date. We're just friends. We hang out together sometimes. We both spend a lot of time studying or working. We don't have much time to date or even meet anyone to date."

"Yea, I just wanted to see the movie, so I called and asked Dotty if she wanted to go. She hadn't seen it, so here we are. You should go with us. It'll be fun."

She looks at Dotty then Jimmy. "Okay, if you're sure I'm not butting in. I've been wanting to see it. I just hate to go by myself. So thanks."

Their pizza arrives, and after they eat, Fredda relaxes some. She feels Jimmy looking at her. She talks mainly to Dotty, trying not to look at Jimmy.

Chapter 102

Dotty picks up on the vibe between Fredda and Jimmy. She sees Jimmy light up when he looks at Fredda. She also notices Fredda is too uneasy to talk to or look at Jimmy.

"Fredda, have you gotten an apartment yet? You were staying with your aunt and uncle."

"Yes, I moved in about a month ago. It's the Highland Terrace. It's nice. It's on the second floor. You will have to come by and see it sometime. I've also got a job as the manager of the apartment. I don't even have to leave to go to work."

"Wow, that's neat. You save a lot of gas money that way. I'd love to see it sometime. Give me your phone number, and I'll call you. Maybe we could get lunch sometime. I work not far from there, and my boss doesn't care when I go to lunch." She takes out her little address book and looks at Fredda.

Fredda hesitates, then looks at Dotty and tells her the number. She didn't want to give it to Dotty in front of Jimmy but didn't have a choice.

"What's your apartment number?" Dotty asks. She figures she might as well get Jimmy all the information she can.

Again, Fredda looks at Dotty and hesitates. "It's 202. I have a nice balcony too."

"Great, I'll call you and come by sometime."

Jimmy looks at his watch. "We better finish our pizza. It's almost time for the movie to start."

Chapter 103

When they get to the movie, Jimmy pays for all three tickets.

Dotty objects, “You were not supposed to pay for mine.”

“Mine either,” Fredda says as she looks at Jimmy.

“Hey, a guy lucky enough to be taking two good-looking women to a movie should pay. Besides, I got a bonus, and I need to spend it in some way. If it will make you two feel any better, you can buy the popcorn. Truce?”

“Fredda, I guess we’re getting the popcorn. We can split it, and get some drinks too. What do you say?”

“I guess we don’t have a choice, it looks like we’ve been set up.”

They get the popcorn and drinks and head to the section where the movie is being shown. Dotty steps aside and tells Fredda to sit down. Then she tells Jimmy to sit down between them since he has the popcorn, so they can pass it back and forth between them. He looks at Dotty, and she winks at him. He smiles at her with his back to Fredda. He sits down. And Dotty sits on the other side of him.

Fredda feels stuck but doesn’t want to make a big deal out of it. She decides to just enjoy the movie, and ignore the fact that he is sitting so close to her.

Chapter 104

As they walk out of the movie, Dotty makes sure Jimmy is between them. "That was a great movie. I love the costumes. They almost looked real."

"Yeah. The special effects are really something. It's like it was really happening." Jimmy looks at Fredda. "What did you like best?"

"I don't know, it was pretty real. I did like the fact the girl got to be the hero. You don't see many movies where the girl ends up being the hero."

"I never thought of that. You're right. It was all good."

They head for Jimmy's truck. Dotty opens the door to get in the back.

Fredda says, "I'll sit in the back."

She gets in, and Dotty gets in the front. "Why don't you take me home first, it's on the way. Then you won't have to double back. It will save you some time and gas."

"Okay, that makes sense. It is a lot closer."

As they pull up to Dotty's apartment, she turns to Fredda and pulls the front seat forward. "You can sit in the front now. I had a great time. I'm glad you went with us, Fredda. I'm going to come and see your apartment the first chance I get. See you, Jimmy, thanks for the invite." She stands there with the seat forward until Fredda reluctantly gets out and gets in the front seat.

Chapter 105

They get back to the Pizza place to Fredda's car. "I'm glad you went with us, Fredda. I haven't seen you at the park lately. Did I do or say something last time I saw you that upset you? If I did, I didn't mean to."

"No, I've just been busy. I don't go as often as I did." She looks over at him and feels a flutter in her heart. "I'm just not ready to get close to anyone yet." She reaches for the door handle.

"Wait a minute, please. I know it's hard to feel like you should not let go of the past, but keep your memories and still live. My mom told me that. She told me Sandy wouldn't want me to stop living. She loved me enough to want me to be happy and find someone to love again. She asked me if it were me that had been killed, would I want Sandy to shut herself off from loving again and finding happiness. I know it's none of my business, but you need to start living again and opening up to people. It's not good to be alone all the time. I guess I should just keep my mouth shut, but I would really like to get to know you better. I think we could be good for each other."

Fredda looks up at Jimmy with tears in her eyes. "I know you're right. I just feel guilty when I find myself having fun, or when I feel myself opening up as I did with you at the park."

"I'm so sorry, I didn't mean to make you cry. It took me getting angry at her for dying, feeling lost without her, and, I guess, hitting bottom when I treated you the way I did at the rehab hospital. It was after that when I finally heard what my mother was saying." He reached over and took her hank. "I'm sorry if I said something I shouldn't have."

When he took her hand, she started to pull it back. It was a reflex. When she did take her hand back, she gently touched his cheek. "You're a kind, caring person, Jimmy. Give me a few days to think about what you said. Your mom is a wise woman." She got out and shut the door. "I'll be at the park next Saturday. If you're there, maybe we can talk. Thanks for taking me to the movie. I enjoyed being with you and Dotty."

Jimmy watched as she walked back to her car.

Fredda felt strange, kind of like she was waking up, and the day was new, even though it was midnight. What was tomorrow going to bring? For the first time in a long while, she was looking forward to it.

Chapter 106

When Jimmy got home he couldn't sleep. He wasn't sure why. He finally got up and took Hero out in the back yard. He sat in a lawn chair and played ball with Hero.

"Jimmy, what are you doing up? Are you okay, or is something wrong?" His dad came out in his robe and sat down in the lawn chair next to him. "I heard you come in, did you and Dotty go to the movies?"

"We went to get some pizza first and ran into Fredda. She went to the movie with us. You remember Fredda. She was a physical therapist at the rehab hospital. She recently moved back here. It turns out Mel is her uncle. She just got an apartment and is also the apartment manager. It's the Highland Terrace."

"Is there a problem? Did Dotty get jealous of Fredda?"

"No, it's just the opposite. She and I are just friends. For some reason, she did everything she could to put Fredda and I together."

"Is that a problem? Don't you like Fredda? It seems like you did everything you could do to get away from her at the hospital Didn't you tell me she had lost her husband in combat? I guess I'm old, but I don't see the problem. You want to talk about it?"

"The problem is I just figured out I really like Fredda. I would like to get to know her better. When we left the movie, Dotty said for me to take her home first because it was closer. I think she just wanted me to be alone with Fredda."

Hero brought the ball back and dropped it at Jimmy's feet. Jimmy picked it up and threw it for him again. He always knows when I'm sad or upset."

Chapter 107

"Anyway," Jimmy continued, "When I took Fredda back to her car, we sat and talked for a while. I told her the same thing you and Mom told me. That if it were me who had died, I wouldn't have wanted Sandy to stop living and cut herself off from everything and everyone. I would want her to find love again.

"I'm not sure if I did the right thing. Maybe I'm butting in when I shouldn't. She said to give her a couple of days to think about what I said. She's going to be at the park next Saturday. She said maybe we could talk then. Now I'm getting nervous. I haven't felt like this since Sandy. I don't know what to do now."

"What do you want to do now? Do you think it could be serious; is that what is scaring you?"

"I don't know what I'm feeling. One minute I want to be around her, and the next, I'm not sure what to do when I am around her. We are so much alike in so many ways. We have both suffered losing the one we loved. I just don't want that to be the reason we are drawn to each other."

"Do you have anything else in common? Does she like the same things you do?"

"That's just it. I don't know what she likes. She likes Hero. She said she always wanted a dog, but never got one. That's about all I know about her."

"Well, then maybe you should find out what she likes. Hero can be a help in that. You said she likes him. Take a picnic lunch to the park next Saturday and take the time to just talk. Not about Sandy or her husband, but about what each of you likes to do. If you find you both like the same things, that's a start."

Chapter 108

Jimmy hesitated, then asks his dad.

"Is that what you did with Mom? Or did you just know she was the one? Like I did with Sandy?"

"I fell in love with her on a blind date. It's just that we were with other people. After the date, I found out where she lived and all the other details I could about her. Then I got up the nerve to ask her out. That was all it took. We've been together ever since."

"Thanks, Dad. I feel better. I think I'm going to take you up on your advice. I'll take a picnic lunch to the park. I just hope she shows up. I might have said the wrong thing. If she does, I am going to find out what she likes. I guess I'll go from there. Right now, I'd better go to bed and let you go to bed, too." They both get up, and Jimmy hugs his dad. "I'm lucky to have you and Mom. You have always been there for me. You let me live my own life, but still watch out for me. I love you both so much."

"We love you too. Any time you need us, we'll be there. Now, you've kept this old man up past his bedtime. Go to bed and leave the thinking until tomorrow. Good night, son."

"Good night Dad. Hero, let's go to bed." Hero takes off for the door and beats Jimmy there. His dad laughs and moves out of the way.

Chapter 109

The next week seems to go so slow. Jimmy thinks Saturday will never get here. He has trouble keeping his mind on studying and work.

"Hey Jimmy, did you hear what I said?"

"I'm sorry, Mel. What did you say?"

"I said that part for the Ford has come in, and it's in my office. Where are you today? It's for sure you're not here. Is something wrong?"

"Nah, I've just got a lot on my mind." He wonders if he should ask Mel about asking Fredda out. "It's getting close to the end of the term and I'm just nervous about passing my exams. Guess I'm kind of freaking out."

"Don't worry, you'll do fine. You have worked your butt off, taking extra classes and pushing yourself. You're a bright kid, ah, man. I know you'll pass the first time. Then you'll leave old Mel in your past and become a big-time attorney. Just don't forget us, little people, when you leave."

"You are really funny. If it were not for you, I wouldn't have had the money to buy my books and the extras. This job got me through. I haven't said thank you enough for letting me have my old job back. It means a lot to me to have you in my corner. You're a good friend too."

“Okay, Let’s not get all sappy on me. You don’t want to see a grown man cry do you?’

“Hey, Mel, phone.”

“Saved by the bell.” Mel laughs as he heads for the office.

Chapter 110

On his way home, Jimmy decides to take a drive and finds himself passing the Highland Terrace apartments. He knows that is where Fredda lives. He thinks about stopping, but she said he needs to give her time to decide what she wants to do, so he just keeps driving.

Fredda is in her office. When she looks out the window, she sees Jimmy drive by. She wishes he would stop, but then she is grateful he doesn't. She is still undecided about what he said. *Am I ready to let you go, Mark? I don't know if I can ever love anyone the way I love you. Would you want me to? Jimmy is really nice. He has lost someone too. Is that why I feel drawn to him. I felt such a strange feeling when he took my hand. It did make my heart kind of jump. I haven't felt that since I met you. I'll just wait until Saturday and see how I feel. Aunt Jackie said I should start trying to live again. Maybe she's right.*

Later that night, Jimmy is in his bedroom and his phone rings. "Hello. Oh, hi Dotty. What's going on?"

"I just called to see how it went with Fredda. I could tell you had a thing for her. I don't think she had any idea. That's the reason I told you to take me home first."

"Yeah, I figured. How did you know? Was I that obvious?"

"It was the way you lit up when she walked in. When she sat down, you couldn't stop looking at her, even if you tried to hide it. I think it's great. You both deserve someone special. You have both been through a lot. Have you asked her out yet?"

"No, we talked a little when I took her back to her car. She said she would be at the park Saturday. Hero and I will be there too. I hope we can talk some more. If it goes okay, I'm going to ask her out."

"I hope it does. Let me know. Got to go. Talk to you later."

Chapter 111

"Thanks for the lunch, Mom. We're going to the park. Be back in a while. Come on Hero, let's go." Jimmy opens the door to his truck and Hero jumps in the back seat. He puts the lunch basket on the floor on the passenger side. "Let's hope she's there today." Hero wags his tail in excitement.

Jimmy gets to the park, and he and Hero find a bench and sit down to wait. A couple of hours go by and still no Fredda.

Jimmy finally gives up and figures she has changed her mind. He doesn't feel like eating the lunch, so he gives most of it to Hero, who will eat anything, anytime.

"Okay, Hero. Let's go home, I guess she's not coming. Hero heads for the truck with Jimmy following.

Chapter 112

"Did you enjoy your lunch?" His mother asks when he walks in the door.

"It was okay. Hero ate most of it."

"Didn't your friend show up?"

"How did you know about Fredda?"

"When you asked for a lunch to take, you asked for some extra. I figured you had a friend meeting you at the park. Plus, you seemed really excited when you left. And would Fredda be the girl we met at the VA? She seemed nice. I didn't know she lived here."

"She moved a while ago. She is Mel's niece. She left the rehab hospital. She manages the apartments she lives in. The Highland Terrace. I ran into her at Mel's barbecue. I didn't know she was his niece. Then when Dotty and I went to the movies, we ran into her at the pizza place right before the movie and she went with us. I thought she was going to be at the park today, but she never came."

"You must like her some. You seem disappointed that she didn't come to the park today."

"I don't really know her, but I'd like to know her better. She seems like a good person. I think I told you she was married and lost her husband in combat. She is like me in a lot of ways. She lost someone she really loved like I lost Sandy. It's hard to think about caring for someone when you think you will never love anyone the way you did before. We talked a little about that. I guess she's not ready to get close to anyone yet."

"Give her a little time, Jimmy. She might want to, but she is just having a hard time letting go. She thought, just like you did, that it was forever. We don't get to control forever. It's not in our hands. You have Hero to help you cope with life every day. If she is alone, she has a harder time getting from one day to the next."

"I love you, Mom. You can see things I can't. I love Hero; he is my best friend. I guess I never thought of him as my support person, but he is just that. I'm very lucky to have him." Jimmy goes over to his mom and hugs her. "But I'm the luckiest to have you and Dad."

"You have no idea how much we worried when we heard you were injured. We are the lucky ones. Some of the injured never made it home. You are the most important person to your dad and me." She looks down at Hero. "And, of course, you too, Hero. We love you for taking care of our Jimmy."

She goes over to the counter and gets a dog cookie for Hero. "This is for being so brave."

Chapter 113

Monday after school, Jimmy is at work. He is bent over the hood working on a motor. He feels someone tap him on the shoulder. He turns around to see Fredda standing there.

"Hi, Fredda."

"Hi, Jimmy. I wanted to talk to you. Have you got a minute?"

He looks at Mel, who is watching them. Mel nods his head.

They walk outside and sit on the bench.

"I just wanted to tell you why I didn't get to the park on Saturday."

"It's okay, you don't have to explain anything to me."

"Yes, I do. I was getting ready to go, and a good friend of mine called. She works at the VA. Her husband had been injured in combat and she was a mess. She didn't know how bad it was and she asked me if I would come and keep her company until they called her back. I didn't have your phone number, and I had to go be with her. I knew what she was going through. I'm sorry. I was going to come. I stayed until this morning with her. They finally called, and he was on his way to the army hospital. She left to go there this morning. He is going to be okay. He was hit in the shoulder by a sniper. He might lose his arm, but at least he's alive."

"I'm so sorry, Fredda. You did what you should have done. She needed you and you were a good friend. I would have done the same thing. What do you say we try it again? How would you feel about having dinner with me tonight? If you're too tired, we can do it another night."

"No, I would like that. Do you know where my apartment is?"

"Yeah. How about I pick you up around seven. That will give me time to go home and get cleaned up. I know you like Mexican food?"

"My favorite. Seven is fine. I can take a little nap and be ready at seven. I'll see you then."

Chapter 114

Jimmy walks back in to find Mel waiting for him by the car he was working on.

"I didn't know you and Fredda were friends. What's going on? Even though it's none of my business, she is my niece."

"Boy, are you nosy. She is going to have dinner with me tonight. Is that okay with you, boss?"

"I guess so. She is very important to Jackie and me, but you are one of my favorite people, so yes, it's okay. Did you know she lost her parents when she was only fourteen? Her father was stationed overseas. Judy, his wife was there visiting him. The base was bombed and they were both killed. Fredda didn't go because her best friend was having a big birthday bash and she wanted to go. That's the reason she worked at the Veteran's rehab hospital. To give back to the ones who get injured. Then she met a guy in the service who was home on leave and lost him also. She is very fragile. If it were anyone else but you, I would worry."

"I'm glad you told me. I didn't know. She is special, I can tell that. I just want to get to know her. We are so much alike. I wouldn't hurt her, Mel. We both have been hurt enough. Now, I better get back to work. I've got a date and my boss wants this finished before I can leave." He picks up his tools and goes back to work.

Chapter 115

"What's the rush?" his dad asks as Jimmy runs in the door and heads up the stairs with Hero right at his heels.

"I've got a date with Fredda. I've got to hurry. I'm supposed to pick her up at seven. That doesn't give me much time," he says over his shoulder.

"What was that all about? He shot up the stairs like he was on fire," his mom asks.

"He has a date with Fredda. Need I say more?"

"I'm so glad. He was really disappointed Saturday when she didn't show up at the park. I guess she had a good reason. I'm glad to see him start to get out. I guess we're babysitting with Hero tonight."

"Looks like it."

Hero is excited because Jimmy is excited. As Jimmy is getting dressed, he tells Hero about going to dinner with Fredda. "You will have to stay here with Mom and Dad. Sorry, but the restaurant wouldn't let you in. We'll make another date with Fredda for the park so you can go. Okay? Now, I've got to go." He and Hero run down the stairs. Hero stops at the door, and Jimmy turns and kneels and loves on Hero. "Be back soon. Thanks for watching Hero for me." He says as he shuts the door.

Chapter 116

When he arrives at Fredda's door, he realizes how nervous he is. *This is a real date. I'm not sure how to act. Get it together, Jimmy. You've been around her before.* He finally gets his nerve up and knocks.

Fredda opens the door. "Hi, come on in." She steps back to let Jimmy come in.

"This is a great apartment. I really should get one for myself. But it's saving me money staying at my parents' house. Every time I bring it up, they say they like having me and Hero around. It was too quiet with me gone. Besides, they have fallen in love with Hero. They spoil him all the time. When Mom cooks dinner, she fixes something for Hero." He realizes he's talking too much, so he shuts up.

"Your mom and dad sound like they enjoy having you around, you and Hero. He's a really great dog. I had fun playing ball with him at the park. Maybe we could do it again sometime."

"Yeah, he'd like that. Maybe we could have a picnic next Saturday if you're not busy. I guess managing this apartment takes up a lot of your time."

"It's not so bad. I have a box for the tenants to put problems in if it's not an emergency. If it is, they can call me on my office phone. I have an assistant who works on the weekend to make extra money for school. She goes to college and it helps her. Plus she can study while she's here."

"That sounds like it helps both you and her. Well, I guess we had better go if you're ready. It's probably not too busy since it's a weeknight." He helps her on with her jacket. Being that close to her makes him nervous. He can smell her perfume. "You sure smell nice."

"Thank you. That's my favorite perfume it's called Lilac like the flower. I've been using it for years. One of my patients gave it to me for Christmas. His wife picked it out for him to give me. She would come to visit and we got to be friends too."

Chapter 117

When they get to Jimmy's truck, he opens the door for her, then gets in on his side. "You are a gentleman, Jimmy. That is unusual nowadays. I had a man in front of me at the store today, and he actually shut the door in my face. Women really appreciate a man that opens the door and does little things for her."

"That's just the way I was raised. My dad taught me to treat women with respect. He has always treated my mom so well. He likes to spoil her. But she spoils him too. You will have to meet them sometime. You would like them."

Dinner went well. They talked like they had known each other forever. They both loved the outdoors and animals. He found himself opening up to her about a lot of things. She, in turn, opened up to him also. They laughed about some things they had done in school and some of their friends. They avoided talking about Sandy and Mark. It was easy to just be in the now.

Jimmy walked Fredda to her door. She unlocked the door and told him she had enjoyed dinner and getting to know him. He said he had enjoyed it also. He asked her about a picnic on Saturday and she said she would like that. She said she was looking forward to seeing Hero again.

Chapter 118

On the way home, Jimmy felt good. He had had a great time. He was also looking forward to Saturday.

When he started up the stairs at home, he heard his mom say good night. “Good night Mom. I guess if I were sixty you would still be waiting up for me.”

“Me and your daddy both.”

“Good night, Dad. Love you both.”

He went right to bed since he had to work the next day. But he couldn’t go right to sleep. Hero was waiting up and didn’t want to settle down. He always missed Jimmy and had to have his share of love before he would let Jimmy go to sleep. Finally, after convincing Hero he was loved and missed they both went to sleep.

Chapter 119

The next day at work, Mel gave him a hard time about taking Fredda out. It was all in fun. Jimmy said he didn't kiss and tell. Mel just smiled and said he was glad they were going out together. But Jimmy better watch his step, he was her uncle, but also he was Jimmy's boss.

Jimmy laughed. "I'm your best mechanic. I can't help it if I'm irresistible" He had to run from Mel, who tried to grab him. Mel just laughed and went into his office.

The rest of the week seemed to drag by. Finally, it was Saturday. He told his mom about the picnic with Fredda and she made a special lunch including some of Jimmy's favorite cookies. When he came down to get the basket, she noticed he had on a new shirt but decided not to say anything. She was happy for him. He seemed excited about life again. After he left, his dad came into the kitchen and said he was happy too. He hadn't seen Jimmy that happy in a long time.

Jimmy and Hero got to the park and found the bench they sat on last time. They had just sat down when Fredda came walking up.

"Wow, that's a big picnic basket. Are you expecting a lot of people? Hello, Hero. I'm glad to see you." She sat down and rubbed the top of his head. He laid his head in her lap.

"No, my mom just got carried away, I guess. I hope you're hungry. She also made some of my favorite cookies. I brought some iced tea to drink if that's okay."

"That's great." She looks in the basket. "She sure thought of everything. Let's dig in. It all looks good."

Chapter 120

After they eat, it's Hero's time. Fredda throws the ball until she feels like her arm will fall off. Hero just keeps going.

"You know as long as you throw that he's not going to stop. He never seems to get tired of playing ball." Jimmy pulls out a blanket from under the basket and spreads it out under one of the trees. "Hero, you need to rest. Or maybe Fredda needs to rest."

"This was a good idea. I haven't had this much fun in a long time. I love playing with Hero. If I had a dog, I would want him to be like Hero. And tell your Mom she outdid herself on the lunch. The cookies are fantastic. I would love to have her recipe. I am stuffed. I enjoy your company too, Jimmy. I feel like I have known you in another lifetime. You know how to make me laugh and it feels good."

"I like being with you too. It's funny that we seem so much alike. Maybe we did know each other in another lifetime. I guess nothing is impossible." He reaches over and takes her hand. "I want to get to know all about you, what you like and what you don't like. I want to spend as much time with you as I can. If you want to. I hope I'm not going too fast. I really like you. I hope you feel the same."

“She looks down at her hand in his. I would like that too. You and Hero have become very important to me in such a short time. I don’t know why I feel that way, but I do.” Hero comes up and drops the ball in her lap, then gives her a big sloppy lick on the cheek.

“I think Hero feels the same way.” He leans over and kisses her lightly on the lips. When she doesn’t back away, he does it again. This time it’s not lightly, it’s more passionate.

“Ah, I think Hero wants me to throw the ball some more.” She has turned a light shade of red and gets up to get the ball. “Come on, Hero, you haven’t worn me out yet.”

Chapter 121

Jimmy watches the two of them together and smiles. *She is something. I think I'm falling for her. I hope she feels the same way. I would like to make love to her. Maybe I'm going too fast. I better back off some. It's just I've been so lonely for so long. I miss you, Sandy, but I need to let you go. I think you would approve of Fredda.*

"I do think Hero would go on forever if I kept throwing the ball. He has more energy than I do." Fredda said as she sat down on the blanket.

"He needs to get the exercise. He stays in the house while I'm at school. When I get home, he is ready to play. Dad likes to play with him, but he wears him out pretty soon. I'm glad he has you to play with. He likes you."

"I like him too. He's wonderful. You're very lucky, or he's very lucky, I'm not sure which." She feels her face turn red; she looks down at her hands.

Jimmy looks at her and feels a funny thing in his heart. He wants to kiss her again but isn't sure how she would react. *Might as well find out.* He leans over and puts one hand on each side of her face and just looks in her eyes. "I'm going to kiss you," he says. When his lips meet hers, she leans into the kiss. She feels it too – the loneliness she has felt and the need for a love she has been missing for so long.

When he releases her, they both start to pet Hero, as a distraction. Jimmy finally looks back at Fredda.

"I think I'm falling in love with you, Fredda. I know we don't know each other well and we haven't known each other very long, but I feel so good when I'm with you. I feel something I haven't felt for so long. I want to be with you. I want to make love to you."

She pulls back and looks at him. "I think I feel the same. I'm just not sure if I'm there yet. I feel good when I'm with you too. Even though we have only know each other a short time, I mean, since I moved back here, and we found out more about each other. I'm just a little scared. Is it because we have, I'm going to say it. Is it because we have both lost someone we loved? Is that what pulls us together? Or is it real, what we're feeling for each other? I don't want to get hurt. If we go that far, then find out it's not what we think..."

"I know what you mean. I've thought about the same thing, but if we don't see where this is going, are we going to miss out on something great. I don't mean we have to make love right now, even though I want to be with you. I mean, just get close enough to find out if it could be a forever thing. I don't want you to do something you're not sure about. I just want to be able to hold you close and know you want to be close to me, too. We can take it as slow as you want. I just know I feel something inside I haven't felt before. I loved Sandy, but I have room in my heart for another love. A different kind of love, but just as deep. I want another life, a home, and maybe kids. I think that could be with you. If you will just give us a chance."

"I would like to have a home, and I've always wanted kids. I want to be close to you. I would love for you to hold me and know what you feel is real. I have thought about making love to you. I have wondered what it would feel like for you to touch me. I'm just not ready to let that happen. Can you give me time to find out what I feel? Find out if it's you, not just that I'm lonely. I haven't been with anyone since Mark. He is the only man I've ever been with. Can you understand what I'm saying?"

"It was the same for me and Sandy." He picks up her hand and kisses it. "I can wait as long as you need. My feelings are not going to change. I want you to be sure. When we do make love, I want you to feel free to love me back."

Hero couldn't stand it any longer. He felt left out. He got up and sat down between Jimmy and Fredda and licked each one on the face.

"I think Hero needs some attention." They both laughed. "It's getting late, too. We could go for ice cream later this afternoon."

"I would like that, as long as Hero gets to go too. I like the package deal. You and Hero. If that's okay."

"I'm getting a little jealous. Hero is getting a lot of your attention. But I can live with that. As long as I get my share."

Fredda leans over and plants a big kiss on Jimmy, then kisses Hero on the top of his head. "See, I kissed you first." She smiles at him, and his heart skips a beat.

Chapter 122

Jimmy sets the basket down on the table and turns around to find his dad standing behind him.

“How did the picnic go? Or should I ask? You have a smile on your face that I haven’t seen in a while. That good, huh?”

“It was great. We had a good time. Hero wore Fredda out, chasing the ball. The food was awesome and so was Fredda. We talked for a long time. I think I’m about to get myself in deep. She is so special. But we’re going to take it slow.”

“That’s a good idea, son. You have plenty of time, so don’t rush into anything. Even though you met her at the Veteran’s hospital, you need to get to know her as a person. She lost someone too. So you both share something. You can build some memories before you go that far. Then if it’s the real thing, you can make more memories.”

“I was thinking about asking her over for dinner Friday night. Would that be okay? I really want you to get to know her.”

“I think that would be nice. We didn’t get a chance to spend any time with her when you were in rehab.”

“Thanks, Dad. We decided to find out who we are as a couple, before going any further.

I'm going, no, Hero and I are going to pick her up for ice cream later. I've got to shower and change. Come on, Hero, we've got to get ready."

"Jimmy is falling for Fredda. I hope she feels the same way. He's on cloud nine." Dad says to Mom as he walks into the den. "He wants to have her over for dinner Friday night."

"That sounds like a good idea. Even though we only got to say hello to her at the hospital, she seems like a sweet girl. I would love to see him happy again with someone who loves both him and Hero. I know he's been lonely; I could tell. Maybe she is the one. I guess we'll just have to wait and see." She puts her arms around him. "Just like you're the one for me and have been for all these years"

"I was the one who had to convince you, I was the one."

She smiles up at him. "You just thought you did; I knew from the start. I just enjoyed watching you trying to convince me."

Chapter 123

Jimmy comes back down and finds his mom and dad in the den. "We're going, don't know what time we'll be back. Love you." Then he and Hero were out the door.

Fredda was standing at her window watching for Jimmy and Hero. She had changed and redone her hair. She had put it in a ponytail. She wanted to look good for Jimmy. *I'm afraid I'm falling in love with Jimmy. I feel lost when I'm away from him. I'm scared when I'm with him. I want to make love to him, but that's a big step for me. That would mean I am sure about us. I want to be, it's just it would mean letting go of Mark. I think he would like Jimmy. He's so nice and a good person. He's devoted to Hero. He wants to get married and have a family, that's what I want. Mark, I love you, but I need to start over. I need to say goodbye to you. Give me the strength to do that.* She sees Jimmy and Hero pull up in his old truck. Her heart beats a little faster as he gets out. *He is handsome too, I'm sunk. I am in love with him.*

Before Jimmy can knock on the door, Fredda opens it. Hero bounds in, and Fredda laughs. "He acts as he lives here. I did put a water bowl out for him in the kitchen. I also bought some treats for him at the store. Is it okay if I get him one?"

“I don’t think he would object. He loves treats. That was sweet of you to do that. You’re going to spoil him more than I do. Can you come to my house Friday night and get to know my parents. They ask about you.”

“That would be great. They seemed nice. Of course, you know Uncle Mel and Aunt Jackie. They think the world of you. We should get together with them too. Uncle Mel knows we’re dating, so I’m sure Aunt Jackie does too by now.”

Chapter 124

She goes into the kitchen and gets Hero a treat. They both come back into the living room. “You want to sit down? Or do you want to go right now?”

“We can sit down for a while, we’re not in any hurry.” He sits down on the sofa; she sits beside him. He picks up her hand and holds it. “I’m getting used to holding your hand. I hope you don’t mind.”

“I don’t mind a bit; I like holding your hand.”

Hero comes up and sits down in front of them.

“I think Hero is getting used to us being together too.”

They sit and talk for a while. Then decide to go get ice cream.

“What kind of ice cream do you like,” Jimmy asks.

“I like chocolate, how about you.”

“I like chocolate too, Hero likes vanilla. I get him a single dip in a bowl.” After they get their cones, they go outside and give Hero his. They decide to go for a ride out to the lake.

“It’s so pretty here. The moon is shining on the water, and it looks like glass. Hero seems to like to just run around. He does have a lot of energy."

They sit on a bench near the water. Jimmy puts his arm around Fredda. She leans into him and puts her head on his shoulder.

"You know, I have decided I am in love with you. I hope it's okay if I just say it. I don't expect you to say it back, I just want to say it. I love you, Fredda."

She lifts her head up and looks into his eyes. "I have decided I love you too, Jimmy. I'm just going to say it. I love you."

He kisses her a deep passionate kiss, which she returns. They look at each other and kiss again. They sit wrapped in each other's arms and watch Hero chase the blowing leaves.

Chapter 125

When they get back to her apartment, she unlocks the door. She turns to him, and this time she kisses him. She starts inside and takes his hand to lead him inside. Hero is already inside.

"Are you sure, Fredda? We have plenty of time. You need to be sure."

"I'm sure, Jimmy. I want you to make love to me. I want you, and I'm sure."

He follows her into her bedroom. Hero starts in too. "No, Hero, you stay in the living room."

Later, that evening Fredda looks up at Jimmy. "Are you hungry?" She asks. " I can make us something to eat." She says as she puts on her robe.

He puts on his pants then follows her to the kitchen. He comes up behind her and wraps his arms around her. "You don't know what you have done for me. I have something to look forward to. I didn't think that would ever happen again.

She turns and kisses him. "I seem to have the same problem. But if you don't let go of me, I can't get anything done. Are a sandwich and chips okay? I have given Hero a piece of ham and a treat. He is asleep on the sofa."

"A sandwich sounds good. What can I do?"

“Get the drinks out of the fridge. The chips are on top of it.”

“I guess I better go after we eat, it’s late.”

“It is late, so why don’t you just stay here with me tonight. It would be silly for you to drive home so late. Hero likes my couch, and I have that big bed.”

“It would be a shame to disturb Hero, he is sleeping so good. And you do have a big bed.”

Chapter 126

“Well, he didn’t forget where he lives,” his mother says as he walks in the front door.

“Good morning. I hope you didn’t wait up for me last night. I didn’t want to drive home that late.” He says with a grin on his face.

“We finally gave up when it got so late. You seem very cheerful this morning.”

“I am. I’m in love with Fredda. And it’s amazing, but she loves me too. I want to bring her over so you can get to know her. I know you met her at the rehab hospital, but you didn’t really have a chance to get to know her. She is going to be around for a long time. I plan to ask her to marry me but we’ll be engaged for a while. I want to graduate and take the bar before we get married.”

His mother gets up and puts her arms around him. “I’m so happy for you, Jimmy. You deserve someone to love you and be good to you. I can’t wait to get to know her better. If you love her, she must be a wonderful person.”

His dad stands and pulls both of them close to him. “I think that’s great, son. I want to get to know her better too.”

“I have an idea.” His mother says. Why don’t we have Mel and Jackie over for dinner Friday night too? Then we can all get to know each other better. Maybe Fredda won't feel like she is put on the spot if they are here."

"That's great Mom. Thank you. I'll ask Mel at work Monday."

Jimmy and Hero head upstairs. Hero seems to pick up on the excitement. He bounces up on the bed and looks at Jimmy.

"We are going to propose to Fredda. If she says yes, we'll be a family. I know you love her like I do. She loves you too. I've got to ask Mel first. I'm going to Monday at work. I hope he says it's okay. I think he will."

Chapter 127

Monday, he gets to work early. Mel is in his office, he knocks.

"Come in, Jimmy, you're here early. What's up." Mel asks.

"Ah, I want to talk to you. You got a minute?"

"Sure. What's going on? You look serious."

"You know I've been going out with Fredda. I want to ask her to marry me. If it's okay with you, you being her uncle. Also, Mom and Dad would like for you and Jackie to come over for dinner Friday night. I have asked Fredda to come to get to know my parents. Could you come? Fredda and I would like for us all to get to know each other better."

Mel stands up and faces Jimmy. "I didn't know it had gotten that serious between the two of you. You haven't gone together very long. Are you sure?"

"Yes, I'm sure. I love her, and she loves me. We are good together. We are good for each other. I haven't asked her yet. I wanted to ask you since her daddy is gone. You are close and like a dad to her. I will be good for her. I want to wait until I pass the bar before we get married. I can take it at the end of this year. That way, I can get a good job and be able to support us. We both want a family too. I can make a good living for us." He stops and looks at Mel, waiting for him to say something.

Mel sticks out his hand to shake Jimmy's. "I think that's wonderful. I know you. You're a good person and will be good for her. I am happy for both of you. When are you going to ask her?"

"I want to take her out to dinner next Saturday, someplace nice. Then maybe drive to the lake. I haven't gotten a ring. That will give me time to pick one out. I guess I'm thinking she will say yes."

"Well, you certainly have my blessing, in case she asks. And I'll ask Jackie about dinner, but I'm sure it will be okay. Now, go to work. It's time to open the shop." He laughs and pushes Jimmy toward the door.

"Thanks, Mel. Who would have known I would end up marrying your niece?"

Chapter 128

Friday night, Jimmy and Hero are all dressed up for the family dinner. His mom has made a special dinner. The dining room is set and the dinner is almost ready.

"Mom, can I help do anything? Boy, this looks so good. You made a chocolate cake too. You're the best." He hugs his mom.

"This is a special occasion. We're going to get to know our future daughter-in-law."

"Well, I haven't asked her yet, but I think she is going to say yes. Mel gave me his blessing. He said Jackie would be happy for us too."

Jimmy's dad comes into the kitchen and hands his wife some flowers.

"What did I do to get flowers?" She asks.

"All of this makes me remember how it was when I had to ask your daddy for your hand. And how lucky I was he said yes." He walks over and kisses her.

The doorbell rings and Jimmy and Hero rush to the door. Fredda, Jackie and Mel were waiting.

"Come on in." He takes Fredda's hand and leads them into the living room.

“Hello, Jackie, Mel. It’s good to see you. We just don’t get out enough, so this is nice having company.”

His mom comes in from the kitchen to greet everyone. “Dinner is almost ready. It’s good to see you again.”

“Can I help do anything? I did bring some cookies I made this morning.”

“Thanks, Jackie. I’ve got everything done, but you can help me put it on the table.”

Dinner goes great. Everyone has a good time. They are having coffee after dinner when Jimmy and Fredda sneak out into the backyard. Of course, Hero goes too.

“I want you to know I am so happy Fredda and Jimmy have found each other.” Mel looks at Jackie. “We are both happy. We think so much of Jimmy.”

“Thank you, Mel. We feel the same way about Fredda. She has made Jimmy very happy. Since they went outside, I guess it’s safe to say I think it’s going to be a permanent thing.”

After everyone had dessert and Mel and Jackie went home, Jimmy and Fredda sat in the backyard again and played with Hero until it was time to take Fredda home.

Chapter 129

Today is Saturday and Jimmy has gotten a ring. He tells his mom and dad he is going to ask Fredda tonight. He has made a reservation at the Italian restaurant that is downtown. It's one of the best restaurants in town.

"Hero, you're going to have to stay with Mom and Dad tonight. I'm going to take Fredda to a nice restaurant for dinner, then we're going to drive up to the lake and I'm going to propose. That means ask her to marry me – us. I hope she says yes. Keep your paws crossed. I've got to go now. Be a good boy for Mom and Dad." He takes him downstairs and his dad gets Hero up on the couch with him.

"Good luck, Son," his dad says.

"You look so happy. I'm happy for you." His mom hugs him. She has tears in her eyes.

Chapter 130

Jimmy gets to Fredda's door, and checks to make sure he has the ring in his pocket. He knocks on the door. When Fredda opens it, his heart beats faster.

"You look beautiful, Fredda. I don't know if I want to share you with anyone. I will have to fight the men off."

"Thank you, Jimmy. You look great too. I've never seen you in a suit. I might have to keep the women away from you."

"Are you ready?"

"You haven't told me where we're going. You just said to dress up."

"It's a surprise. I wanted to do something special for you."

When they pull up to the restaurant, the valet comes out to park the truck. He opens the door for Fredda, then takes the keys from Jimmy and gives him a stub for the truck.

"Wow, Jimmy. This is nice," she says as they enter the main dining room.

"I have a reservation," Jimmy says to the man at the door. "Jimmy Johnson."

"Yes, sir. Right this way, Mr. Johnson." He leads them to a table by the window. "Is this satisfactory, sir?"

"Yes, this is great. Thank you."

Their meal was very good. They talked and laughed. He couldn't quit looking at her. The black dress she had on looked like silk. He noticed it fit all of her curves and had a neckline that showed just enough. He thought about how lucky he was to be with such a beautiful woman – the woman he was going to ask to be his wife. After dinner as they got in his truck, he turned and kissed her.

"I thought we could drive to the lake. It's such a beautiful night. Would you like that?"

"Yes, I don't want this night to end. Let's drive to the lake."

Chapter 131

Jimmy stopped at the top of a hill overlooking the lake. The moon was so bright and shown through the trees. He got out and opened the door for her. They walked down to a bench and sat down.

"You have made me so happy, Fredda. I know I was a jerk when we first met, and you forgave me. I never thought you would be the one I would fall in love with." He took her in his arms and kissed her that kiss she had learned to love. He was so gentle yet passionate.

"I never thought I would love again, Jimmy. But you have broken through all of my walls. I didn't stand a chance. You made me fall in love with you. And I've never been happier."

He got down on one knee and pulled a tiny velvet box from his pocket. He opened it up and pulled out a silver ring with a diamond in the middle.

"Will you marry me, Fredda? I love you and will always take care of you. I will be true to you. I will do my best to make you happy."

She sat there for a minute with a startled look on her face. Then she got up and knelt beside him.

"Yes, Jimmy, I will marry you. I love you too."

He put the ring on her finger and kissed her. Then he got up and helped her up and kissed her again.

"It's beautiful, Jimmy. It fits perfectly. How did you know what size?"

"I looked at your hand the other night, and I looked at my mother's hand. I asked her what size she wore and went from there. I'm glad it fits, and I'm glad you like it."

Chapter 132

They sat back down on the bench. He had his arm around her. "I also asked your Uncle Mel if I had his permission to marry you. He said yes. He was happy for us. I told my mom and dad I was going to ask you tonight. They want you to come for dinner tomorrow. They are anxious to get to know you better. They like you already. Hero knew I was going to ask you, he was glad. He loves you."

"I love Hero too. I want to get to know your parents better. I know they raised a good son. I would like to tell them that. Uncle Mel thinks the world of you, you know. He said that when he found out we were dating, he hoped it would go well. I guess it did."

"I would like to wait until I pass the bar to get married. I can take it at the end of this year. Then I can get a good job and be able to take care of us. If that is okay with you?"

"Yes, that's a good idea. You can concentrate on your studies, and I know you will pass the bar. You're not only handsome, but you're smart. And I'm glad you're mine."

Chapter 133

The end of summer finds Fredda and her Aunt Jackie looking for a wedding dress for Fredda. The search seems endless until, at a little boutique downtown, she finds just the right one.

“Fredda, that is the one. You look beautiful. The lace around the neck is so dainty, and it matches the lace on the sleeve. All we need now are shoes. You are going to look perfect.”

Jimmy has passed the bar and has an offer for a job at a local law firm that is very prestigious. He accepts the offer. All his hard work has paid off. It’s two weeks before he and Fredda are going to be married. They have decided to try to find a small house not far from his work. She has given notice at the apartments. The final day comes.

“I am so nervous, Aunt Jackie. Do I look all right? I want to look perfect for Jimmy. I love him so much.”

“You couldn’t be any more perfect. Mel is waiting to walk you down the aisle. Jimmy is waiting at the altar. I am so happy for the two of you. You both deserve to be happy.”

She can hear the wedding march as they near the door to the chapel. She sees Jimmy standing there waiting for her, with Hero by his side, waiting for their life to start. Jimmy turns to look at her. When they reach the altar, her Uncle Mel takes her hand and places it in Jimmy's hand.

A Second Love begins.

* * *

Sharon Allen

Sharon lives in the country with her husband Dale. She enjoys working in the yard and writing. She has several animals, all of them rescues.

Her romance books include: *The Swing*; *Two Hearts, Two Loves; A Second Love; Is His Love Real; A Broken Love; and My 3 Loves* with more in the works.

Sharon also writes children's books which include: Cloie's New School; Jake: Homeless to Hero; Charlie's Dream, Lizzie to the Rescue; and I Danced With My Daddy.

Her books are available as ebooks and paperbacks on Amazon and other platforms.

Made in the USA
Coppell, TX
28 July 2024